THE

Lamp Post

❖‹‹❖‹‹❖‹‹❖‹‹❖

THE Lamp Post

MARTIN GREGOR-DELLIN

*Translated from the German
by Richard and Clara Winston*

New York: ALFRED·A·KNOPF

1 9 6 4

c. 3

L. C. catalog card number: 64–17702

This is a BORZOI BOOK,
Published by Alfred A. Knopf, Inc.

FIRST AMERICAN EDITION

Originally published in German as *Der Kandelaber.*
© 1962 Walter-Verlag Olten und Freiburg im Breisgau.

NOV 9 '04

BL

To MY FATHER

THE

Lamp Post

After having survived a Nazi concentration camp, Teacher Blumentritt
finds himself bound by comparable
restrictions in Communist East Germany, but is constantly reminded of
threats against individual liberty
by a lamp post on which the Nazis
hanged a man.

THE morning the anony-
mous letter arrived, snow
was falling. The clock in the Fish Market grew a rind of
white. The square was crisscrossed by paths of slush from
tramping feet, but at the center all the diagonals swerved
away from the black lamp post. Before Blumentritt left
the house, he took the mail from the letter box. There
was only a blue-gray envelope. He carried it back to his
room to examine it. No return address, cheapest kind of
paper, addressed without street number, badly typed on
an old typewriter, the letters irregular. He could make out

3

the Schochern postmark; it was a local letter. His cane already in hand, Blumentritt lowered himself into a chair, thrust his stiff leg under the table on which the remains of his breakfast stood, and opened the envelope. He took out a sheet that had been carelessly torn from a pad of graph paper and folded once. The typewritten lines ran across the sheet, crookedly, unevenly spaced. He read:

We are aware that in your classes you glorify the new order go on doing so and suck up to them we wll take note of these methods and warn you where they lead. You, whose father was a decent man, ought to be be ashamed. Have you sold out? If so consider that we know plenty about you that might make you trouble.

There was no signature. Blumentritt looked up from the sheet of paper and stared vacantly at the spot where a beam jutted from the window wall into the room—the house had thick walls. Then, with downcast eyes, he returned to the writing. When he had read for the third time that his father had been a decent man and that he ought to be ashamed, he folded the note and slipped it back in the envelope. It was ridiculous to speculate about the author of the letter. There was no sense taking the thing seriously; best to forget all about it at once and completely. He thrust the letter into his coat pocket and left the house.

Blumentritt was always balancing on an unsteady tightrope, one leg in the air, mists beneath him concealing the solid ground or else an abyss, who could say; the mists

kept everything hidden; you could never see more than a
small part of a whole. He balanced as if a rope were
stretched across Schochern from one side of the valley to
the other and he teetered along it when he moved between
his apartment on the Fish Market and the school where he
taught. His way led down Monastery Street and Peace
Street, across the Bridge of Friendship, up the Boulevard
of Progress to the Fairy Fountain. All the way to school
and even during class he could not manage to blot out the
question of who could have written the anonymous letter
—*methods and warn you where they lead.* One of his
pupils, one of his colleagues? One of the parents of a
pupil? Someone who knew him, someone who did not
know him?

During the first hour he took care to call only on
Blümel, Timm, and Zeymer. He never had any trouble
with them; they knew what was wanted and believed in
nothing. He did geography; he pulled down the green
map showing the brown lung of the Harz Mountains, on
the right the red-rimmed aorta of the Oder, the branching
blue veins of the Elbe. Name the western tributaries of
the Elbe. The big map drew the pupils' attention from the
teacher. He could let his mind ramble while Zeymer
rattled off the names of rivers, could brood over the various
possibilities: someone obviously wanted to intimidate him
by sending the letter, but who could it be—all these years
he had kept his mouth shut. His pupils understood him;
they seldom embarrassed him. Aside from Schunke and

(5

Fenk. But the letter could scarcely have come from them; they considered Blumentritt too reactionary (what was wrong with the guy, what did he have against gunnery?); they watched him closely, drove him into corners, set traps for him. This was easy enough when he explained history in general terms, steering away from the set formulas of the textbook and the newspapers. Still and all, the letter writer could not have been one of his pupils. Then what about Frau Luja? He did not believe her capable of it; they had too good a relationship, although they spoke very little to each other, confining themselves to essentials.

His train of thought was cut off by a commotion in the class. Zeymer had made a mistake in the rivers—where was the Wilm—the thin vein grew thicker from bottom to top of the map, not the reverse. The laughter, once it had erupted, was difficult to check; until the end of the hour Blumentritt had to concentrate on maintaining discipline. By the time he was called in to Kumtsiel, after the lesson, he had almost decided to hand in the anonymous letter, as was proper. But he did not, although he could not have said why.

Principal Kumtsiel was called Kumt for short—it meant "horse collar" in the local dialect. He wore a gray suit, white shirt, and gray tie; his face, soft and good-natured, with heavy pouches under the eyes, drooped twisted and askew beneath his high forehead and big, bald head. He took the largest hat size among the faculty; an informal

survey had once established that. Some years ago the
local newspaper had carried an article about him. The
clipping, framed, hung beside his desk. It read: When I
wanted to see him, a meeting of the party leaders happened
to be going on, so of course I could not disturb him, but
he said he would be at my disposal afterwards. Why do
you want to write about me in particular, he asked; I
don't do anything special; it's just this way: in years to
come our children will be what their teachers, their
school, and their education system have made them; our
teachers have a great responsibility, for they are educating
a younger generation whose perspectives—and so on. It is
highly significant that Norbert Kumtsiel has continued
deepening and reinforcing his education. Today the
teacher is assuming the leading role in the instructional
process as representative of society . . . a new and wider
field of socialistic pedagogy and the progressive traditions
. . . a tribute to his social conscience, his abilities as educator . . . and so on.

This article, including a picture of Kumtsiel—the photograph was deeply smudged in reproduction—hung in the
principal's room. Kumtsiel was in general a social person
who wore no party badges and was moderately strict.
With the pupils he occupied a middle ground between
being popular and being despised; their private name for
him was Dopey. He deliberately overlooked Blumentritt's
physical handicap, the principle being, if I assume him to
be totally fit, I can demand more of him—he therefore

did not offer Blumentritt a seat. Blumentritt wondered why he had been called to the principal's office, where the reports from below and the instructions from above met at the green desk top.

"Is the Fenk affair still simmering?" Blumentritt asked. Kumtsiel sat behind the desk. "I hope you're not going to make new difficulties for me."

"You had to reprimand him, I grant."

"He was disrupting the class. It was in self-protection, that's all."

"All right," Kumtsiel placated him.

"Since we're not allowed to touch the pupils, I had him leave the room."

Kumt pushed himself back from the desk and looked out of the window. "That was just what his father fussed about. In his letter he complained about reactionary methods, refusal to teach."

"I couldn't do anything else."

"The case is closed—don't worry about it. But this other matter . . ." He broke off, moved back to the desk again, and continued: "It's very awkward, but I must speak about something which concerns you personally."

"What is it?"

Kumtsiel shifted his shoulders back and forth, but his bald head remained in a fixed position. Blumentritt noticed that his shining pate cut off the lower edge of the official portrait on the wall, that of the patron of youth, hiking, heavy industry, sports, the arts, agriculture, and literature.

The triangle of the latter's beard rested its point on Kumtsiel's head. Kumt took his time; he found answering hard.

"There are, er—" he cleared his throat "—certain questions in regard to your associates."

"My associates?" Blumentritt shifted the weight of his body from his stiff leg to his sound right leg. "Would you mind explaining."

"It concerns only one person," Kumtsiel amended. "A woman, you know—we understand one another?"

Blumentritt did not reply.

"You are maintaining these ties with—with a woman from exceedingly bourgeois circles. Why don't you legalize the relationship? Or even better, put an end to it—yes, that would probably be still better, all things considered." But of course, he went on, that was only a recommendation, no more; it had just occurred to him; his attention had been called to the matter, and it was not really important, not at the moment, anyhow. "Nothing to waste much talk on," Kumtsiel assured him. And since Blumentritt had not yet replied, he was forced to speak more plainly: "Of course I have heard some talk about 'putting it to him squarely.' You know the sort of thing. But there's no need to dramatize these things. I'm just passing on what I've heard, in a friendly way."

Friendly? Blumentritt thought.

"I cannot imagine that any serious charges can have been raised against the person in question."

(9

"No, no, God knows—if there is a God—I didn't mean
it that way." Kumtsiel shook his head back and forth; the
beard on the wall danced on his bald pate.

"And what is *bourgeois* supposed to mean? Do you refer
to her parentage? After all, her father was put in charge of
municipal archives after the war."

"Yes, quite right, of course. How could I have forgotten
that? Is he still alive, by the way?"

"He is, but she doesn't live with him."

"She has her own house?"

"Out on Crooked Hill."

"If I remember rightly, there was once an unpleasant
business with her first husband—in that house." Kumtsiel
stood up and perched himself on the edge of the desk.

"Is that what you were getting at?" Blumentritt asked.

"It just occurs to me," Kumtsiel replied with a miserable
attempt at offhandedness, "that there must have been
something to the story. He or his brother was a Nazi, and
I thought that you as an anti-Fascist . . ."

"All that has nothing to do with her, and both brothers
are dead. Let's be frank! Was this business started by
Mayor Heiland? You know that the mayor lives in the
house next door to her . . ."

"What makes you think that? Nothing of the kind.
Heiland? This—but I've already told you, my attention
was called to the matter and I thought it advisable to inform you of certain questions that were raised. In all
friendship. After all, the teacher today, as the representa-

tive of society, has a great responsibility for—ah, you know well enough."

"My personal affairs are in order, and as for my teaching . . ."

"Yes, yes, of course." Kumtsiel wearily twitched the furrows in his soft, wide, blubbery face, which now had a yellow look, as if poisoned by tobacco fumes. "And since we happen to be speaking of Heiland: a notification will be sent through the classes an hour from now. The school is marching in a body to the induction; the senior classes are being given their labor assignments. The mayor will speak. Tell the boys to behave." Thereupon Blumentritt took his leave; but at the door Kumt called after him: "And don't worry about Fenk. The matter is closed."

Blumentritt left him, a weary man who no longer bore the slightest resemblance to the model educator of the newspaper clipping.

In class—Blumentritt went through irregular verbs—he again began to experience the odd and unaccustomed sensation that someone was pointing at him. A letter, a threat . . . what did it all mean? He had the boys write on the board: *Ich darf, du darfst, er darf, wir dürfen.* Perhaps the criticism came from the parents' advisory council. No, he could not fix on a definite suspect. And besides, Kumt was right on one point: there was no need to dramatize. I point, you point: Timm, write it on the board. Only when the conjugation was all written out did Blumentritt realize that it was a regular verb. He had to consult the grammar book to find a suitable example, so distracted was he. It was a welcome respite when a student came round with the notification.

Heiland winds up his speech. The pupils' clapping flutters up to the stage. I must try to retain the meaning of his words, for I shall have to discuss the speech in class—I've forgotten completely—what did he say? As though I did not understand the language; it's always the same, and then one day I catch myself mouthing the same phrases. So I've probably listened after all. I deceive myself. Deceive myself about myself; I probably listened just now, too, and followed every word. Heiland has left the stage, but the outlines of his face are still sticking to the wall like a transfer: that cone of a head, like a piece of wood turned on a lathe, with the gray, bristly, close-cropped hair, the blue, moist, birdlike eyes, the thick glasses with their dark horn frames, and the glint of yellow incisors, so large he can scarcely close his lips over them. The applause dies down; the induction ceremony for the boys continues.

From right and left the stage fills with blue-clad men. The lectern has been removed; the women's chorus disappears from sight behind the men. Three lines of men move to the front and weave about; their regular tread thumps across the floor of the stage, wafting dust into the dimness of the hall. The audience is briefly intrigued, then drops

away again into indifferent vacuity. The chorus can no
longer be seen, but this is not a slip-up in the arrangements.
No one imagines there has been any slip-up, neither the
students down in the auditorium nor the parents in the gallery, nor I. The chorus has fallen silent; so has the
orchestra deep down in the narrow gorge in front of the
stage. The lights of the music stands make points of brightness behind the wooden partition. The illumination on the
stage is increased by a few watts; the bulbs glow more
brightly; the stage manager pushes the lever down a little,
but the blue figures absorb the light so that it comes to the
same thing. That is how it is with the apparent slip-up,
too; you can depend on something to adjust it, eliminate
it, balance it, for along with everything else the whole
course of this morning's program has been carefully
planned and fixed beforehand. The wings shake under
the tramp of boots. Above the men's shoulders, rifle straps
tauten; the stubs of the barrels protrude a finger's length
beyond them. In addition to the rifles, the men have
leather belts; the blue uniforms are one-piece affairs,
simple tubes which are puffed out by air at every step.
Five hundred pairs of eyes note the rifles on the stage and
the marching men behind the draped proscenium, and this
impression is filed away in the brain like a document whose
disposition is not yet decided. If only what is supposed to
happen on the stage would become clear. The rows of
armed men move together from left and right and form a
solid group which marches in place, with rhythmic up

and down movements of their feet. A command to halt; the feet strike the floor once more; then the whole formation faces about, toward the auditorium. A curt command and the conductor in the orchestra pit raises his baton. And now—perhaps the violinists are just lifting their instruments to their chins—a sudden movement, an unexpectedly sharp noise, startles everyone. Just above the orchestra pit, up front near the footlights, the first row of uniformed men lunge forward and throw themselves down on the stage, their rifles crashing loudly as they hit the floor. At the same moment the second row drop to their knees and raise their rifles; behind them the third row continue to stand in a firing position.

The short stubs of the barrels, the dark small eyes of the muzzles, extend over the edge of the stage and point, a whole line of them, into the auditorium. From up front, from my position, what is seen behind the rifle barrels are the flat, foreshortened heads without chins, pressed against the butts; the fingers can just be discerned, crooked on the triggers, and the raised feet, tilted to the side. Between the men in the last row the white blouses of the chorus gleam again. Everything has been carefully rehearsed and proceeds step by step; no question of a slip-up. The conductor gives the signal. The cues are clear: command, drop to the floor, music. Now the national anthem is hurled above the guns into the auditorium, the menacing boastful words supported by the exclamation marks of the music. Song and weapons fuse. I think about the students:

which one's finger mentally crooks on the trigger and which one draws back in fear. But they seem to be merely surprised, that is all. The end of the meeting is near, and they are hungry. Perhaps the scene that now takes shape means nothing to them. The scene: the slender violin bows below the cold metal of the gun barrels, moving rhythmically up and down. Each time, just before the bows reach the height of the stage, they withdraw again to the depths of the orchestra pit. Bow and metal almost touch, and almost without a sound; for the violins are drowned out by the chorus; the singing roars out of the background, tossing arches of triumph into the air. Vigor and victory blare from every throat; shudders run down our backs; no one is completely immune. It comes in waves. Blasts of the tuba, trumpets and horns. What do they need the fiddles for? They might have saved themselves the trouble. Heiland made his speech. But the thought of Heiland does not prey on my mind, for I am more concerned with the boys, who give no sign of their feelings. Their heads are tilted back, the napes of their necks pressed into the chairs so that their weedy growths of hair tumble over the tops of the seats. I am sitting with my class. I know these boys, I see them every day, but the faces are unfamiliar to me, alien. The boys are pressed back in their seats, motionless, although their rapid, shallow breathing belies the impassivity of their faces. Even when I close my eyes I feel the pulsations around me, the fevered life of the class. They have put on masks for the fun of it. Behind those expressionless faces are swarming thoughts of who stands where in the athletic league, of lunch, of motorcycles; their feet are not still for a moment, their fingers drum on their knees. It is the old story, I know all about it from thousands of hours in school—yes, it must run into the thousands by now. . . . Times that the tension crackles betweeen me and the tamed horde on the benches; and more, when the unspoken, the implied, gathers like a thunderstorm punctuated now and then by the lightning-flashes of bold questions, so that I encourage the discharge of the tension by joking. (Meanings lurk behind every word. Every illusion is dangerous. If I say: "Even Caesar made mistakes," some will gloat and others look askance.) We seesaw constantly between complicity and misunderstanding. Occasionally I yield to the questions; then again I apply the brake by coming out with some official formula. This disappoints many of them, but Schunke, the district attorney's son, looks mollified. Whom do I satisfy? Not those who articulate their doubts within the framework of the curriculum and the ideology, and not those few either who keep on hoping I will go beyond these limits.

All this consumes my strength, and yet it also raises it to a high pitch, an indispensable drug, and the only question is how long the heart can stand it. But it means life and confirms my sense of being. Silence is far more difficult to bear, the moments of emptiness, loneliness. When I am alone, no resistance challenges me; there is no wild herd of young bloods to be tamed for their own good. The interplay is lacking, the resistance that I can lean against and that often sustains me. When I have bent their questions aside and cleared a pathway, a pathway into their selves, I know they trust me. Then they enclose me like a wall and hold me fast. I feel sheltered only when I am among them. Of course they slip away from me again, are lost to me anew every day. All very well. Probably that is a law of nature. But I win them back again, every time. I'm not the only one they slide away from in that way—and that's a comfort. I'd sooner see them independent and quickly slipping away from me than dominated by anyone; if it weren't for their independence I wouldn't be able to bear times like this, when firing squads form up in front of them and the chorus strains its throats to produce a superhuman volume of sound. So much noise awakens my suspicions. What are they trying to drown out?

In the old days the People's House was called the Municipal Theater. But aside from the name, nothing has changed; the old seats are still here, and the floorboards dip just the way they did before the war. When the doors open for a latecomer, a sharp draft blows in. From the ceiling hangs the many-branched crystal chandelier that in my childhood always made me dream of swinging my way up to it on a swing and then rocking back and forth across the auditorium, hanging from it by my arms. I loved to imagine how the crowd would look up at me; joking and frightening them by turns, I would watch the shadows

(17

of smiles and fear chase across the pale faces of my audience.

I enjoyed such fantasies, and if I really consider the matter, I liked to laugh a good deal. It was simply the taste for farcical jokes that led me one day to take part in a fairy-tale play called "The Kidnapped Princess." It dealt with elves and wood sprites, and most of the performers were girls and grammar-school pupils who were used as dwarfs. No one from our class in the Gymnasium volunteered, of course, and I would not have raised my head when the notice went through the classes inviting us to participate, if they hadn't suddenly begun to talk about music. They needed musicians to sit in the orchestra pit and accompany the play-acting. I was always a bit of an amateur musician; I used to fool around with one of my classmates who was a good pianist. Melzer—that was his name—had a sense of humor, too. Both traits brought us together. And when Melzer and I heard about the musical side of the play, we looked at each other over the heads of our classmates. Up went our hands. Five sheets of music, five different pieces, including one by Chopin. Melzer sat at the piano, shaking with muffled laughter that netted him nasty looks from the princess. I had two music stands in front of me, and sat on a revolving stool, swerving back and forth between violin and cello—only by these acrobatics could we imitate the various voices of an orchestra. It was right here in this theater, in this very orchestra pit. We'd switched on the lights of five of the music stands, so that it looked as if half the orchestra pit was occupied, and we played the king's funeral march on the lower registers of our instruments and the wedding polonaise on the upper registers. The princess' name was Inez. Dressed in veil and wreath, she trod across the stage over our heads, her eyes downcast. Although the thing had its funny side, I succumbed to her lure; I fell in love with Inez, although of course she did not deign to look at me. Chopin prelude: wreath, crown and head held high, braids of hair thick enough to tie a man up with, crimson mouth. The dwarfs trembled at every step she took, for her frail self repelled evil although it attracted it—after all, the story dealt with an abduction. But as soon as she left the stage, the proceedings became ludicrous. A plucking of the strings—the king sobs. Melzer quavered down the octaves, and the stool whirled. Would Melzer still remember it? Melzer had moved to parts unknown, his laughter following him. If he still goes on playing quavers today, what does he think of me? Probably nothing good.

Does he know that Hanfstengel, too, is still alive—whom we used to find so comical? Hanfstengel was not only a champion of healthy living and dress reform, but also a canary breeder and a prizewinner in his field—in short, a revolutionary. We made his acquaintance in this theater. Every time "The Bird Peddler" was played, one of Hanfstengel's specimens would be among the players. He lent the troupe a yellow singing canary in a bird cage. In return he was allowed to sit on a garden chair to the side of the stage, where other theaters have their proscenium boxes. He would watch the performance from here, anxiously keeping an eye on his bird. That was the only privilege he was granted during the Nazi period. He lost his posts in the breeding associations and the conservation society, including the one in the Canary Club, because some of his pamphlets and leaflets were found to contain semi-Marxist ideas. After the war he entered the party of general and complete progress, in the faith that a more healthful mode of life, both in dress and nutrition, could best be achieved through class struggle. The party did not reject him. For a while he was permitted to carry on, but on the whole the thing was a misunderstanding. He talked too often. He became a pest at meetings. When expropriations were discussed, he went off on a rant about stiff collars, and when party functionaries started going back to neckties, he ostentatiously appeared in coarse-woven blouses. He bitterly fought the ban on nudism—though not for any selfish reasons, surely, for he was small, stoop-shouldered, and unprepossessing. He had enough of a dwarf's appearance to call attention to himself everywhere. At any rate, he made his fuss and was expelled from the party. The only privilege left him was that of attending performances of "The Bird Peddler" seated on a garden chair to the side of the stage—he does it to this day, and I imagine what he would be thinking now if he were to see the row of sharpshooters sprawled out on the forestage, aiming at the auditorium above the violin

bows which glide back into the orchestra pit each time
they reach the height of the stage. And now the men in
the first, prone row leap up, and the kneeling marksmen
also. That is the final tableau: the chorus standing with
hands clasped behind the rows of the platoon; they march
out to the side; the banners in the background become
visible once more: Down with . . . and Forward to . . .
and Bring on . . . I'd like to know whether good old
Melzer would be able to extract a little comedy from
these inscriptions (I can hear those chuckles of his that
started up from his chest and flooded through his face).
For we, with the best will in the world, can no longer
make out what we are moving forward to and what is
being condemned. Instead of laughing, we try honestly
to understand, for we have ideas about it, but we lack the
imagination.

Between the Fairy Fountain, near which the People's
House was situated, and the Fish Market, Blumentritt's
life swung monotonously and hazardously back and forth.
At times Blumentritt digressed to Karwenka's Art Shop,
where Inez waited. As soon as he reached the Fish Market,
he could no longer escape the lamp post. In his room, when
he stepped up to the tall window, the two-tined fork thrust
itself before his eyes. The lamp post was not very high
and the light it gave was insufficient for the Fish Market.

A good many points could have been made against it, such as that it had been erected in the eighteen-seventies, so that its ironwork was completely out of keeping with the half-timbered gabled houses. But to Blumentritt only one argument counted. That was an image, a memory: the lamp post had once served as a gallows. It stood too close to his window, and was a perpetual reminder of the irrefutable, the irrevocable event of the hanging. Again and again he would drift to the window, only to be stopped by an upsurge of horror. The lamp post made any stay at home an imprisonment; it troubled his reading and threw him off his desk work whenever he had to look up and caught sight of the iron pole with its two arms, which bent slightly downward at the ends, with its glass globes surmounted by sheet-metal shades—they looked like the nipples on baby bottles, Inez said. Evenings, the light from that black lamp post fell into his room—dim, inadequate light, corpselike light—and by day the pole cut the Fish Market into two halves. In the left half stood the Town Hall, where all complaints came to rest. He could not look out on the square in front of the house when children were playing there: tug-of-war and tag and prisoner's base, when they barged into the lamp post shouting, "Safe!" and formed a chain around it—onesy, twosy—or leaned against the pedestal ornamented with iron flowers: last one home is It. Of course they didn't know its history, and in winter looked up at the light as if it were the sun. But he couldn't stand it, couldn't, though there was no evading it. Wherever he turned, wherever he sat in the room, the hanged man drooped outside his window.

He had done enough to get rid of the lamp post, at any rate had done his best, had written a great deal, drawn up petitions. No lack of perseverance on his part. Did he lack support? The truth was he'd found nobody else willing to put his signature to the letters; no one else found the gallows too close for comfort. Frau Luja, who took such excellent care of him, mistook his jumpiness for dissatisfaction with her apartment, and tried to make up for that by even greater services. She responded to each complaint by preparing special dishes for him, by finding a store that sold fresh fruit under the counter, or locating a good supply of real coffee. These things were not what he wanted. Such appeasements devalued his protests; it almost seemed as if he were angling for extra favors.

Frau Luja liked to sing. He might easily have gained his peace, for when he seemed ill-humored, on days when he was irritated by bureaucracy or incidents at school, she would stop her singing. Otherwise she sang in her apartment; he could hear her in the front rooms which he occupied. *Ich kann nicht bei dir sein, muss in die Welt himein*, she sang; *Schifflein, Schifflein auf blauer Flut*. Or: *Wer hat dich, du schöner Wald*, and her voice, always somewhat too high, always a bit off tune, mingled with the strains from the municipal loudspeaker, which came in from the square. If he had said to Frau Luja: I can't stand it any longer; this flat drives me crazy—if he had said that,

(23

he would probably have silenced her, but not the everlastingly unchanging, regular succession of records from the municipal radio: *Auf, auf zum Kampf, zum Kampf.* Or: *Der Graf von Luxemburg hat all sein Geld.* Or: *Du lustiges Rotgardistenblut.* So what would he have gained? Besides, Frau Luja would only have been frightened, afraid that he might leave her and another tenant would be assigned to her—Heaven help us, things always change for the worse. And so he left matters as they were; he didn't want to make things unpleasant for her; they'd grown accustomed to each other and he knew she was satisfied with him, as a tenant.

But he had given up hope that Frau Luja would ever really understand him. She was not capable of that. The whole situation was too unfavorable. Frau Luja's rooms were on the courtyard side of the house. She had been there since the beginning of the war, moreover. Once he had spoken with her about the Incident. She had changed the subject, gone on about her deceased husband—a chance to produce the late Herr Luja's kidney stone, which she kept in a ring box, resting on absorbent cotton, and showed to every visitor. All conversations between her and Blumentritt took place in the hall, or at any rate as they stood. He could never persuade her to sit down; she feared the noisy creaking and groaning of her corset. When talking with him, she clasped her hands over her enormous bosom. Standing so, with no expression of emotion, she listened as he explained that something must be done to make the city remove that decidedly outmoded, ugly, and inadequate street light. Frau Luja seemed not to hear; she bolted into her kitchen, and not until the next day or the day after did he hear her singing again: *Wer hat dich, du schöner Wald.*

And what about the others? Everyone was afraid to get mixed up with public affairs (everything was public) or to put down anything in black and white. Moreover, the tenants in the houses adjacent to the Fish Market no longer talked about the war and its horrors, about executions and the dead. If they were reminded of such things, they waved it all aside, as though saying: "We have troubles enough in our lives." They tilted their heads to one side and finally said: What's that, Herr Blumentritt? Good God, man, that's nothing you want to mess with. Haven't you heard what happened to So-and-so? What became of So-and-so? Let well enough alone, Blumentritt! . . .

Useless to try to explain it to them; they lived in the present, which was dreary enough, they said. Sometimes he thought he detected the trace of a smile on their faces, and when he turned his back to them they said (he could swear it) that he was "turning his back on reality." But what was reality?

The gallows went on standing outside his house. The sight of it unnerved him. Even finding different lodgings wouldn't help. It would be self-deception to escape the lamp post that way. Any kind of outwitting would be a

compromise, and compromise, he believed, always cor-
rupted. After that, he could never come to a genuine
accounting; all that would remain for him was capitulation
and self-sacrifice—thus far ran his rather complicated
logic.

Nevertheless, and this is the moment to admit it, he
had tried to make this compromise. He was prepared to
betray Frau Luja and find other lodgings. He carried
on his search in secret, hardly believing that it would
succeed. He had put in a request for a change of residence,
and he could easily foresee the difficulties it would en-
counter. New quarters were scarce, and people stuck fast
to their old ones. But if an apartment did become vacant
—tenants having moved to parts unknown, or fled, a
punishable offense by present law—swarms of applicants
were waiting for it. At first he received no reply; after
all, he was one of those who was adequately housed. Then
he made his request with greater emphasis. He wrote asking to be assigned another, even if smaller, place in "a
quieter part of the city." He stressed the factor of quiet-
ness. In the long run, he wrote, a teacher who was also
engaged on a scholarly project could scarcely work where
there was so much hubbub, traffic, public radio music,
parades, and often even a carousel going. Besides the
municipal radio there were other loudspeakers, like the
one in the shooting gallery. He had not put down: I
can't stand the lamp post. No, he had not put that down.
But didn't they know that, as a result of his petitions to

the municipal government? The housing office, figura-
tively speaking, was not a stone's throw from the mayor's
office.

Why had he shifted the whole blame to the traffic
and the hubbub, as if that were the difficulty? Hadn't
he become accustomed to all that? Gradually you learned
to live with the noise as if it were an animal threatening
the house, pounding and gnawing in the walls, stirring in
new places all the time, a daily challenge to a wearing
struggle, but at least something you could confront. No,
the noise was not troublesome, or only in a minor way.
The image was, the gallows; there was no way of grap-
pling with its silent existence.

The complaint about the noise was a self-deception, he
knew. He was only running away. But since the running
away was itself a lie, a second, smaller lie no longer mattered.

Now at last, word had come that his case "was under
survey," and that his apartment would be "inspected in
the course of the investigation." What did they want
to inspect? Of course the inspectors would not be greeted
by the full salvo of noise, by the loudspeakers of the
municipal radio with their: *Hat all sein Geld verjuxt,
verjuxt,* or with the song about the man like an oak and
perhaps we'll all be corpses tomorrow: *Da steht ein Mann,
ein Mann, so fest wie eine Eiche.* But one kind of noise
would be enough, the perpetual racket of the shooting
gallery: Bang, bang! He's won again, great, wonderful.

(27

. . . And if the singing in the kitchen (*Wer hat dich, du schöner Wald* . . .) ceased, and the trumpeter no longer died his merry little death, then there would still be the hullaballoo from the Wheel of Fortune: Step up! Join the crowd! Take your chance!

The character of the songs, the blare of the radio, the banners with slogans—only the lamp post had not changed. All the rest was new in Schochern, and was not good. Would he not have done better to leave town? But he was not in the same situation as Melzer, who had begun to interest certain organs of surveillance (or so he had maintained before he cleared out). Blumentritt could not have produced any cogent reason for leaving. He stayed where he had been born and had lived for a long time, as though this clutch of old houses held him in their grip, and the old cobbled pavement, the mist-filled meadows by the river, the rush of drains, the one-way streets, the geometry of history: Tilly slept here, from this point Blücher looked out over the Wilm. Corners that gave back the echo of footsteps. There had been much building and rebuilding in Schochern, but the new had not extended very far, the old peered out here, there, and everywhere. Real excellence in this part of the country seemed too brief, like a sheet that covers only the trunk of a corpse and lets the rigid feet and the stiff blue fingers protrude. It would not seem unnatural for someone already dead to appear on the scene, or for the clay-faced invalids of thirty years ago to be sitting on their stools by the curb once again, mouthing and mumbling together. Even the view down from the castle was still the same —more will be said about this castle shortly. You looked down on the roofs of the town, which had somewhat darkened in the interval; on the woods by the river, slightly thinned, with dense flocks of starlings. On the outskirts of town the brickyard seemed (like all brick-yards) as if it had just been closed down, or were being torn down. On the right side of the valley the Steep Field opposite the railroad embankment, that precipitous slope on which the children would sled in winter, al-though sledding there was prohibited. A barbed-wire fence cut across the hill halfway down, a dangerous fence which had slashed the throat of many a child. As far back as Blumentritt's own schooldays a notice, what they now called a notification, would periodically go the rounds, carried through the Gymnasium classes by the janitor, and read aloud by the class teacher, Dr. Grünmeissel: Sledding on the Steep Field is prohibited from now on (for the how manyth time from now on?). And while the janitor took his departure, Dr. Grünmeissel, to fortify what he had read, jerked his head up and sent a blazing look over the assembled class: You hear that, boys! To this day the principal's office continued to send the same notification around the classes—Blumentritt taught in a grammar school, but in this matter the schools were all alike—only Dr. Grünmeissel was no longer at the Gym-nasium (nor was the Gymnasium called Gymnasium any more); but Grünmeissel was still alive, of course; he was, incidentally, almost the only one of Blumentritt's teachers who was still living. Under his white teacher's tunic Grünmeissel had usually worn uniform trousers and boots; the pupils had called him the oldest Hitler Youth, in the days when membership in the state youth organization was not obligatory. (It had recently become obligatory again; only nowadays the uniform was blue.) The nickname emerged shortly after the incident with the half-Jewish boy in their school. Grünmeissel would begin every school day by announcing the results of the previous day's marksmanship test. "Schmolke: forty-two rings. Bronze medal." Or something of the sort. "Spameital: so many rings for that boy. What are you, Spameital?" That question, curt, almost whispered, stern. And Spameital sprang to his feet: "Youth company leader, Comrade Grünmeissel!" To this the teacher responded: "Very good! Silver medal." His head jerked violently to one side, he performed a rapid about-face on the ball of his right foot, leaped up to the wooden platform, reached for the chalk and the yardstick. Once again that blazing look, chin taut. Grünmeissel was the Schiesswart for the entire town, that is, in charge of all marksmanship practice. Often, to the delight of the class (but what a delight!), half the hour would go on reading out the scores; but the disappointment afterwards was bitter, for all the work they had missed had to be made up. Grünmeissel would hastily slap a few formulas on the blackboard, outline the problems he was assigning, and everybody would have to struggle through the lesson at home.

But no, Grünmeissel was no longer around, although he was still living, although he had a job somewhere and might even be employed as a substitute (for teachers were in demand) to teach arithmetic and the elements of geometry—no more. In short, Grünmeissel no longer played any part in the life of Schochern; but another man was still in the picture: old Metzeki, one of the town's more whimsical characters; the dead pipe hanging at a slant from the old man's mouth, a smell of tar and tinder emanating from him. You met him everywhere you went; the street urchins ran after him calling, "Grandfather Metzeki, your kids eat a lot," just as they had done in Blumentritt's childhood. Generations remembered him, as though he had been around since ancient times. He haunted the dreams of those who had grown up in Schochern—dreams were what bound you to Schochern and did not let you go; it was not the town, that heap of stone and mortar, but the dreams you had dreamed there, those dreams of terror and desire, conjoined with a ray of moonlight that crept through a gable window into a boy's room, when behind a boy's closed eyes an image rose that prefigured in a single moment a whole life, even if it were wrong, perhaps just because it might be wrong. That you will never escape, Blumentritt; you never outgrow childhood.

The war had destroyed his childhood home; a heap of

rubble along the river marked the site. Everything had begun there, but the world was a vast and audacious dare you had to meet. He had gone to Munich and studied under Professor Koram—did anyone still remember him? The way he went on, undeterred by the newly nationalistic state, talking about Christianity's capacity for spiritualization? Political and social thought are branches of humanism! he had taught; the spiritual can no more be separated from the political and the social than culture from the humane. People might not yet see it, but the spirit was already coming into its own, was once more charged with the duty of telling good from evil; reality was making that question easy. . . . Blumentritt had taken all this down, and expatiated on it—many notebooks full. And then: One must know what exists! Professor Koram had maintained until he was arrested right in the lecture hall. Blumentritt and some friends plotted ways to rescue the professor; they conferred, met in various apartments at night, never twice in the same place, and the last time, during his absence, Blumentritt's room was searched by the Gestapo. He left town at once, but they had only been waiting for that. In Schochern, in front of his parents' house, two men in leather coats served as reception committee. What a dreary, unimaginative detail, two men in leather coats waiting at the door late at night. He did not see his parents again, did not guess that he would never see them again; the house in which they slept was the last he saw, and to this day he occasionally dreamed that he stood in front of the house and could not get in. Waking in the morning after such dreams, he would want to get up and go there, but then he would realize that the house was no longer standing. Since it had vanished along with his two parents, they still lived on in him; there was not even a grave in the cemetery for him to visit.

As soon as he thought of the house, memory overpowered him: a flood of scenes, childhood nightmares, autumnal colors seen through the small bull's-eye windows in the workshop which looked out over the Wilm. The dead body of an animal sometimes floated downstream. Once a servant girl came running out of the house next door into the yard. The rush of rain in the roof-gutter, his father poking in the drainpipe, lightning striking across the river. Billows of steam in the laundry room, a hunchbacked cleaning woman helping out, suds running down her big red rubber apron. Most of the time the apron hung on the wall. Once he hid behind it when his father was looking for him—he had broken a tool. He thought of the low, crammed rooms of the apartment, which stretched in a single line from the dark front hall to the bank of the river; of the stairway with the life-sized figure of a sentinel hunched in a corner, holding a lantern over his head; the lantern was lit day and night, for otherwise eternal blackness would have prevailed inside the house of Instrument Maker Blumentritt, who could trace his family back to the Middle Ages; he was proud of his lineage and had his family tree painted in large, neat letters on a plaque which hung beside the piece of statuary in the hallway. Instrument Maker Blumentritt had been a taciturn, almost grumpy man who never showed his feelings. No one knew what he thought and felt about his life. Bottled up in himself, an early riser, never sick and harshly scornful of illness in others, with the expression of a rejected child around the corners of his mouth, dogged about his work and seemingly unaware of the way the work was slowly swallowing him, or the way his treasures, old engravings, furniture, pictures, heaped up around him. All that had gone up in flames—the house so stuffed with things that there was no clear passage, its ancient timbers dried out like tinder, and when the bombs fell nothing could be saved. The thought of how it had happened obsessed Blumentritt; no one had been able to describe it to him precisely; it was just as inconceivable as the happenings in a crematorium. Unfortunately, when Blumentritt crossed the Bridge of Friendship and turned into the Boulevard of Progress every day, he passed the mound of rubble by the river, passed the sparse remains of the foundations, which seemed to him much smaller than the building that lived in his memory.

Officials of the Housing Bureau do not necessarily smell of cloves. But when Frau Luja opened the heavy oaken door, which always stuck a little, she admitted nothing

else but the smell of cloves and pepper, which preceded
the two men from Housing. He saw them crossing the
threshold in their gray-green suits and heard the floorboards creak, as they creaked every time one stepped into
the apartment. He no longer noticed it when he himself
entered.

The head of the Housing Bureau had deigned to appear in person. A small, hollow-cheeked man, he was too
important to introduce himself, and since Blumentritt
could be nobody but Blumentritt, not a word was spoken
at first. His skeletal assistant, with the lidless, inflamed
eyes of a convict who has sat too long in the "hole," at
once set to work. (But which of the two smelled of
cloves and pepper?) He inspected the apartment, while
the head of the bureau moved about vaguely, looking
at the walls, the books, the pictures, the framed photographs, at all these small, individual possessions of Blumentritt, as though these and not the apartment's size and
location would determine its suitability. Blumentritt felt
tempted to launch into a running commentary on all
these objects, like a guide in a museum; the bureau head's
gaze had been resting on them far too long. But this was
neither the time nor the place to speak of Braque and
Chagall, or to identify the photograph of a poet; why
should the Housing Bureau care? Meanwhile the assistant measured the room; he paced it in long strides, taking each step with intense deliberation, poising on one leg
and then plunging down so the floorboards boomed, each

time jerkily and gaspingly counting: one, two and three and four. He checked his measurement again and repeated: one, two and three, four.

It did not bode well when the head of a government bureau kept silent, and this one did. Blumentritt tried to draw his attention away from the pictures. "Do you remember? I wrote to you about the noise . . ." But the bureau head continued to nail the pictures fast with his gaze, or by suddenly lowering his head and drawing in his chin to virtually tear them from the wall. Blumentritt was sorry that he had not taken down the Braque and Chagall beforehand: was it likely that the bureau head would favor styles of art condemned by the official view? On the contrary, it was to be feared that the hollow-cheeked man's decision on the housing question would be adversely affected by Blumentritt's pictures. "The noise," Blumentritt tried to explain, "is often so unbearable that I cannot work."

"What kind of work?" the bureau head asked in a stern, matter-of-fact tone, without taking his eyes from the wall.

"Correcting notebooks, as I am doing now, or working up subjects for themes, marking exams, preparing lectures for the Cultural League, and the disturbance comes not only from the Muncipal Radio . . ."

"Do you have any objection to it?"

Why should Blumentritt become involved in a debate on the usefulness of public radio loudspeakers? Or give his opinion on the selections they played! The apartment was what mattered. Or was a change-of-residence request linked with one's attitude toward these musical programs? "It's the sheer volume of sound," Blumentritt said. "We also have the wheel of fortune and the carousel, not to speak of the shooting gallery. At the moment only the shooting gallery is open; the radio isn't on."

"There you are," the bureau head said.

"But that's exceptional. I only wanted to repeat that I'm not concerned about the size of the apartment."

Now, for the first time, the bureau head met his eyes. "All right," he replied after a pause. "Just the same, the apartment has to be measured."

Blumentritt ventured to shake his head, although he was more inclined to laugh. He told himself: you might have known there would be no point in complaining about the noise.

The assistant was now pacing out the width of the room. He began at the door and counted up to the window: one, two and three and four. Then he turned, pivoting on one foot, and looked back over the distance he had covered as though his measurements would have inscribed themselves in chalk upon the floor. Evidently obeying a sudden impulse, the bureau head abandoned his quiet, waiting attitude and thrust his head forward toward the assistant. Somewhere in the vicinity of the curtain, which the assistant was brushing with his shoulder, must be the reason for the bureau head's unexpected behavior. He trotted over, stooped, tapped the windowpane, and said: "Double window!" He spoke the words in an almost choked voice, as though ashamed of divulging such an obvious piece of evidence. "Double window!" he repeated.

That, Blumentritt realized, was the verdict. The two men also went into the adjoining room; but the procedure there was much abbreviated. The assistant measured the distances only with his blood-shot eyes, whispered one and two and three, then stepped back, no longer needed, to enter all the facts on paper. The head glanced into the next room and concluded: "The width is the same."

"But my request has nothing to do with the apartment's size," Blumentritt objected once more, without hope.

The two men posted themselves in the middle of his study. Blumentritt still could not say which of them smelled of cloves and pepper; but it did not matter, for they belonged together. "They are two fine rooms," the bureau head declared. "Very fine rooms—you can't get around that."

"Granted." The first noonday record was being put on at the Town Hall; it was *Der Graf von Luxemburg*, which meant that this time he would hear of the sad end of the little trumpeter only toward the end of the series of records. "I haven't ever said that the rooms were bad."

"Moreover, we have no doubt that your past record entitles you to this apartment."

"That's beside the point. Do you hear that? *Hat all sein Geld verjuxt, verjuxt.*" Blumentritt gestured toward the square, although he had actually passed beyond disgust. "So what if he's thrown away all his money." He turned away.

"I suppose you don't like music," the bureau head said. The smell of cloves grew stronger; the bureau head had obviously fortified himself with mulled wine to face the rigors of field work.

"You see, I can't concentrate with that going on."

"I understand." The bureau head let his lower lip droop, as though he recognized that his whole visit had been pointless. The assistant meanwhile opened the door. The small, hollow-cheeked man assured Blumentritt once more: "We will give it our consideration." Blumentritt knew that his request was as good as rejected.

After the men had left, he resigned himself to the situation, even felt a certain peace of mind, for now he no longer needed to lie. He no longer had to pretend that his grievance was the noise when the real thing was the lamp post. His petitions could be honest once more; but what was the use, if they brought no result? He had gathered the copies of all his letters in a single file. He had explained that the electricity failed when high winds battered the lamps against the iron framework; he had complained about the expense to the town for repairs, about the danger of accidents and consequent lost hours of labor; and finally he had written about what he had seen and experienced, and what was really preying on his mind.

In these letters he did not use a dry official style. Instead, he tried to give impressions, sketch scenes, couch his story in some graphic form, in order to put his point across. In general he admired evocative prose—all the more so since he had no talent for it; he was not much of a storyteller. When he tried to do anything of a literary nature, he found that he could only dash down the outlines of his scene, block in the essentials. He could not handle details. Of course he had tried; only recently he had tried again to set down one such impression, a triviality, but one worth preserving, one which had forcibly affected him: the image of a street with a pregnant woman standing in it. Houses, a village. A street receding into the flaming evening sky; dust on the street; a dog running through the gate into a yard, the view extending on into infinity. That was how it had struck him, as he rode past. Another scene: a boy at a pond; he had lain here with his girl, although as a matter of fact the girl had been a good deal older than himself. The man remembers: the frogs croaking, the whole thing in the far distant past, and now he stands here again, the frogs croaking and splashing into the water. He takes a stone and pitches it after them. (He had recently taken both vignettes to a printer; he wanted to have printed copies to give to Inez and a few others; after all, he did have a little vanity.)

Enough—writing was not his forte; a new form would

have had to be invented for him; everything that was still in the future he would have described as if in the past (for wasn't the future already determined?), and what had happened or had been could only be rendered as conjecture in the future perfect tense. . . . He confined himself to his letters and petitions. All petitions were sent to the same authority, which remained mute; all written matter was submitted to the man who held the reins of the town in his hand, whose small, moist bluebird's eyes could see into all the offices of the town, who said of himself that he had a low membership number and a high mission: mayor, orator, and veteran party member, the man in the Town Hall.

Carnival was coming. The Party Committee had settled on the slogan: Sure enough! Every year there was another slogan; they couldn't keep the one for last year, for that had been simply "Gee!" and had run into opposition from the churches. There was general reluctance to shout it in chorus. Of course, a few people standing by the curb while the carnival parade passed by (the whole thing consisted of two floats from the People's Rubber Factory), a few people had shouted it, of course. But it did not sound right for the progressive achievements of the People's Rubber Factory to be hailed with halfhearted adolescent cries of "Gee"—halfhearted because the churches had publicly announced at Sunday services that the word was a distorted appeal to God. So when people yelled "Gee" in the dance halls, in the streets, and at the transfer of the keys in front of the Town Hall, they did so with a guilty conscience. There had been no intention to call upon the Lord's Son; the Party Committee had goofed badly there. To be sure, the cry of "Gee!" to express consternation or amusement was common in Schochern. People sometimes said "Gee-whiz" and held their hands over their mouths when they made a mistake, when the milk boiled over or a dish fell into the toilet. But there was a difference whether the cry just slipped out of you or whether you yelled it deliberately and in chorus (thou shalt not take the name of the Lord, and so on, the ministers said on Sunday). In short, the first carnival cry had been a bad mistake, and this time the Party Committee issued the watchword: Sure enough! Those words were to dominate the two days of the week-end to which Carnival had been shifted so that the holiday would not interfere with the work week. On Saturday small paper hats and big noses could be seen in shops and offices, and from behind displays of knitted wear and cake boxes, from behind cheeses and gory butchers' counters rang the greeting: Sure enough! Spoken not very loudly, rather the way people wished each other good morning. Only the hundred per cent orthodox could boom out: Sure enough! And who was in that category? Out on the street the greeting was generally omitted; even

at carnival time people don't like to make fools of themselves on the street; you might as well expect them to
do a headstand and walk on their hands down the Boulevard of Progress. No, people in Schochern were not
carried away that easily. They opened their mouths re-
luctantly anyhow: a torpid and clumsy bunch, the Party
Committee spluttered whenever it thought of the regular
demonstrations in the Fish Market. It was always the
same: at each demonstration the compact squads of march-
ers approached from all directions, from all the side streets;
but when they reached the square the rear ranks dissolved,
seemed to get stuck in lanes and alleys or to adhere to the
corners of the houses, and in the end it was only a paltry-
sized crowd that occupied the square, and stood there
heavily in the rain of sound falling from the Municipal
Radio. Nobody opened his mouth. It had been the same
way in the thirties, when the Führer's deputy had come
there. In Schochern everything went off differently from
the rest of Germany; there was always some embarrassment connected with the visit of the second man in the
state. To be sure, the streets were densely lined with people, the Fish Market browned by uniforms—in those days
the Fish Market was not called Fish Market, but it wasn't
called that nowadays either; only Blumentritt called it by
its old name, and why should we not go along with him?
—an open black limousine drove the upright effigy with
the heavy eyebrows into the center of town. But the
swarming crowd kept silent. The high official's right arm

went up and strained backwards, crooked until the back of his hand almost touched his shoulder, as though he were carrying an invisible tower upon his palm. But silence. The blocks, walls, and clusters of people remained still. A few random "Heils" sounded from the lamp post, from the two-tined street light on which several boys had hoisted themselves; but the shouts quickly subsided, ashamed of themselves. The chief deputy's eyes burned from under his heavy brows; he streamed his aura in all directions, but nothing happened, not even when he reviewed the troops.

And now the same apathy at carnival time! No matter what kind of show was put on, there was no turnout, nobody wanted to stir. That was how things were in Schochern.

The two floats loaded with the costumed members of the youth organization rolled toward the Town Hall at the scheduled time in the evening, but the Fish Market was deserted. The Municipal Radio started up. The young people on the floats sang; their outstretched arms waved greetings to nobody. Girls, chilly in their tight bodices, huddled closer together. Skin gleamed between bright cloth and gold braid. On the platform in front of the Town Hall a microphone stood ready. The floats stopped; the Council of Eleven and the Girl Guards mounted the wooden platform; but just as the Carnival Prince began his speech, the municipality switched off the electricity. This was a common occurrence in winter and of course no spite was intended; the power plant obeyed higher orders. Blumentritt, at the window of his room, found the speech inaudible, and could not see a thing; probably the participants themselves could not see anything. The Carnival Prince talked into the darkness. Here and there a few lighters and matches flared. Candles were lighted behind several of the windows on the Fish Market. Somewhere to the side of the platform—impossible to make out just where—a reddish glow flickered. It came from a side street; something, probably of paper, had been set on fire there. When the short-lived blaze was over, the square was wrapped in darkness once more; nothing could be seen or heard of the whole tomfoolery. Then, after a quarter of an hour, the electricity came on again; the street lamps flared and all the windows in the Town Hall were brightly lit, although the offices had long since been closed. At the same time the record player started up—it had been switched on as a precaution when the floats arrived, but to no avail. A record of laughter had been put on; the laughter reverberated over the deserted square. The record played itself through again and again and went on even while the boys and girls gradually trickled away. Singly and in groups they disappeared; their task was done. But the jollity of the record was inexhaustible; from the loudspeakers of the Municipal Radio the laughter echoed, bubbled, spluttered, sighed, faded, and began again, booming, bubbling, spluttering. The walls threw back the echo; the floats and costumes were long since forgotten, but still the record ran on. Blumentritt stood at the window and stared down at the deserted square, in which nothing was to be seen, until at last a pedestrian came along; he crossed the square from the right, with coat collar turned up, head bowed under the torrents of laughter from the loudspeaker. Blumentritt waited until the solitary walker, who did not look around, had vanished around a corner at the other end of the square.

It seemed that what had been burned was a poster, and the episode was not without a sequel. A search for the malefactor was conducted in the schools. "You must have seen who was responsible!" Blumentritt was told. "You were closest to the scene." But how could he have made out anything in total darkness? He thought it best not to allude to the failure of the electric power. "The glow of the fire came from a side street," Blumentritt explained to the faculty, "and I don't even know whether anybody from our school participated in the carnival activities. It certainly wasn't a large turnout." Kumtsiel groaned under his responsibilities as principal. "Leave it to God, insofar as He takes care of anything," he said; and after the conference he spoke to Blumentritt privately: "Have you considered what I said to you recently? Think of socialist morality and draw your own conclusions. You should stick with your kind of people in your private life too." But who were his kind of people?

. . .

The musical bell on the door of Karwenka's Art Shop was somewhat out of kilter. Of its triad, only the tonic and the fifth were left. The bell tossed an abbreviated greeting at the entering customer. The name of Karwenka on the brittle, weather-beaten door frame, white script on a red ground, was only a leftover; it had nothing to do with the present owner. After Karwenka's death the small shop had stood empty for a time, until Inez Keil took it over and filled it with antiques that her father, Archivist Meiran, had given her after her husband's suicide. With them she was to start an arts and crafts shop, and thus relieve her financial difficulties. It had been painful for the archivist to part with these possessions and in his heart he still mourned for them—those that had found buyers. A few remnants, bits of porcelain, pewter pitchers, a chipped sculpture of African or Melanesian origin, an old mantel clock, were carried along hopelessly from inventory to inventory; in Schochern there was no demand for such things. More to the point were salt shakers and other small gift items which filled the glass case at the rear of the shop: wood carvings, peasant pottery, wall decorations, handmade toys, pretzel stands, carved bowls and bookends. The African sculpture, a totem with two figures one atop the other, the lower about as tall as a medium-sized flowerpot, the upper somewhat smaller, was Blumentritt's favorite piece. He liked the two long-nosed midgets who held their arms akimbo. They stood in the show window, a greeting to

(47

passers-by who had a feeling for that sort of thing. Blumentritt had it, at any rate; he could not look at the figures without smiling. When two figures were as similar as these two, an element of parody was involved. The statuette was not for sale, any more than the picture of the Uffizi Gallery on the wall and "Woman Arising," a stone figure, approximately life-size, by the hand of the now deceased sculptor Kummerbart, who had made his home in Schochern. "Woman Arising" had remained as a monstrous heritage of the Karwenka era; she weighed at least a ton; and no one wanted to face up to the task of removing her from the shop to some site where she might perhaps do more honor to the memory of Kummerbart. So there she stood, one foot forward, a basin in front of her, next to the counter, opposite two wicker chairs which Inez had brought from home. When you sat in those chairs, you looked up at the stone chin of "Woman Arising." Her step forward seemed doomed to frustration in the small space of the shop. The basin in front of her remained hovering between giving and taking, undecided. When you stepped through the door you felt, for a moment, that she was lunging at you.

To the accompaniment of the broken tinkle of bells, Blumentritt stepped out of the damp coolness of the March day into Karwenka's shop. Dry fragrance of wood greeted him, and a trace of perfume. Little Frau Zergaden, a creature withered to hermaphroditism and with a vaguely epicene attractiveness, without a waist but with a gently

curving bosom, gave him a glance and then vanished behind the green burlap curtain that separated shop from
office. She knew whom Blumentritt had come to see—
and seemed to disapprove. He sat down in the wicker
chair beside "Woman Arising" and waited for the burlap
curtain to be parted again. It was violently wrenched
aside by a thin, nervous hand. Inez entered, leaned against
the counter, and drew her mouth into a smile which
might mean: It's you! She propped her chin in her hand.

Alongside "Woman Arising," the excessively buxom
Jugendstil monster, she seemed almost frail—although she
was hardly so. The impression of frailty vanished when
you looked at her for any length of time. She had full,
well-shaped hips; her shoulders had no trace of boniness;
her hair fell long and uncurled down to them. What made
her look so evanescent and at the same time attractive
was the undisciplined grace of her movements, a certain
abandonment, and then that apparently so uncomprehending, innocent, startled look in her eyes. As she looked,
she might keep her mouth open and her head tilted, as
though she had never heard anything about the world and
the mischief-making race of creatures that disported itself
therein. But a moment later, by a surprising forward
thrust of her chin, a word, a single yes or no, she would
make it plain that she saw through many things much
more rapidly than others. All that, her childlike curiosity
at times, her capacity for enthusiasm, her way of tossing
back her hair to reveal her high, smooth forehead, and

(49

her gift for pretending, for playing innocent (playing the princess, for example, with eyes downcast)—all that hovered on the border where girlishness passes over into hysteria. She also had something of the nun about her. As a matter of fact, she had been at a convent school in Erfurt, but had run away in the dead of night and come back home. Her father, what else could he do, had made a stab at putting her over his knee, and had then sent her to the girls' secondary school, the lyceum, in town.

When Blumentritt had seen her as a girl that first time, her hair was in a braid, the weight of dark hair hanging down in a single heavy plait to the side of her head. Her posture was poor—she stooped so much that she seemed almost hunched, and when she was greatly excited she would pull her braid forward and sink her firm white teeth into it. In the upper classes of the school she had been the topic of unsavory gossip and rumors: Who had made her? Who went to the park with her? But few of the stories had withstood examination. It was true that she went around with venturesome boys of dubious reputation; but she always held back enough to feel the pleasant sensation of being herself. And if the boys became too enterprising, an astonished look of wide-eyed innocence would stop them in their tracks.

During the war she came into contact with foreign workers—that was what they were called, although they were really prisoners—and at times felt a dangerous urge to "plunge," to try out other forms of existence. She wanted to feel what it was like to work in the fields beside barefooted girls, to stand in the rain and be wet to the skin, to wear the same rubber raincoats as the Polish slaves at her side, with the rain streaming down her body as it did down theirs. But she knew all the while that she was safe; she could leave it all behind her and forget the crude obscenities she heard; she did not have to sleep on straw, even though it tempted her. One day she perhaps stood around too long with the Poles, so that she was suspected of having become involved with one of them. Her father, the Archivist, got her back home just in time, before they shaved her head, and she married a shy, colorless man of forty, Benjamin Keil, a treasury official. Inez marrying him! people said, and wondered whether this might be another of her experiments with new kinds of life, even though this time it was for keeps.

But it was not for long. Benjamin Keil came into a small inheritance along with his brother, Paul Josua. On Crooked Hill they built themselves two houses side by side, as alike as a pair of twins. Paul Josua and Benjamin were in fact twins, though their characters differed radically. Benjamin was pale, bespectacled, timid—in fact, permanently intimidated. Paul Josua was the exact opposite; he had an urge to be in the public eye, liked to cause talk, liked to have a hand in everything. It was not his way to do his duty innocently and unassumingly like Benjamin, the treasury official. Timidity was not one of his failings; he had lofty aims, wrote highly emotional tracts on religion and

Bibical criticism, predicted this or that divine judgment, and was frequently asked by nonsectarian families to deliver funeral speeches in which he would inveigh against sensual pleasures. But in time he tired of this sort of thing. The audience for such stuff was falling off; even in Schochern, times were changing, after all. Apocalyptic warnings were no longer in demand, and so Paul Josua fabricated a new faith for himself; he no longer quoted from the Bible, but from a Household Book of Nordic Maxims and Proverbs, with neo-nationalistic and racist overtones. Paul Josua was not exactly a strapping specimen of the master race; he never wore a uniform and did not even belong to the party. But he discovered the beauty of the swastika as a type device, and used it liberally in all his printing jobs. He obtained a respectable position in the municipality and became indispensable during the war —a fact which proved his undoing in the year of the defeat. Whom had he antagonized the more in his life: the Christians or the non-Christians? He had been mixed-up. At any rate, the Christians denounced him to the Occupying Power, and the Occupying Power, composed of decided non-Christians, dispatched the visionary into the hereafter by way of a nearby concentration camp. Paul Josua did not return from the camp. His house was confiscated, and soon the new mayor of Schochern moved into it. That was Heiland.

But this was by no means the whole story. It seems that a tree stood on the boundary between the houses of the two brothers. It was a cherry tree. Paul Josua was long since dead, but the question of the ownership of his property had not been really clarified—at least, so Benjamin thought. He wanted some cherries for Inez. He was always very attentive to her. Oddly enough, they remained childless. The cherry tree stood, to be exact, in the adjoining garden, or almost so; the fence was right up against the trunk, but the roots were also on Benjamin's land. Moreover, most of the branches overhung Benjamin's garden. Why should he not pick a small basketful? As far as he was concerned, it was still his brother's cherry tree. He set up a ladder and had mounted it when Heiland's voice struck him, quivering in the air like a piece of cracked metal: "Keep your hands off them!" No more. But the words got under Benjamin's skin. They remained hanging in the air; they pursued him everywhere, and they seemed more dire with each passing day. What might happen? Would he lose his job? His house? Sink into poverty? What might there be in his personal file, what incriminating evidence against him might be left over from his unfortunate brother? He kept indoors and stayed far from the window so that Heiland could not see him. But what good was that; he could not sleep nights for fear. In any case, he had the habit of sitting for hours on a chair, his weak and anxious eyes staring into space. Now that grew worse. At the office an important job was coming up, the examination of the books of a factory. If that job wasn't assigned to him, if it were taken away from him, then it would certainly mean, he told himself. . . . Or should he take the bull by the horns? It would not help his case to cringe and wait to see what happened, he decided. He would try to close the incident, would apologize; he was ready to humiliate himself, if that was what was wanted. He found out what time the official car came to pick up Heiland at the Town Hall. One afternoon Benjamin trudged up and down in front of the Town Hall gate, waiting. The car drove up, Heiland left the building, crossed the sidewalk in three strides, and started to get in. Benjamin went up to him—Heiland was already seated—stooped under the roof of the car, and asked for an opportunity to clarify the misunderstanding. But the door slammed, the car started; he stood alone.

Next morning he was relieved of the task of examining the factory's books. Perhaps that was—but who could say, in hindsight? Benjamin asked for an appointment at the Town Hall, was not received. He waited until Sunday morning. Then he left his house, turned left at the garden gate, and rang the bell of the house next door, which he had so freely entered when his brother Paul Josua was alive. A rash and senseless act—for Heiland would not even admit his neighbor. He had no business with him, he called from inside the house, and his voice shook; if there was anything to settle, he said, it would be done in other quarters. He did not wish to be bothered at home.

In other quarters? That could mean one thing and another, possibly everything. Benjamin went back to his house and kept silent throughout Sunday dinner. After dinner he lit a cigar and said he wanted to look up some old files. Inez lay down for a nap. When she awoke, it was late afternoon. She called Benjamin, but there was no answer. She looked for him all over the house. Then it occurred to her that he was poking about in old files which were kept in the attic. Mounting the steep staircase, she saw, between the joists, first his feet in the air, then his body, then the distorted face. It was all alien to her.

Blumentritt knew all that. The tale of the two brothers was one of the town's favorite stories, richly elaborated. A few talks he had had with Inez long ago, but never resumed, had only served to dispel various details invented by the Schochern mythic spirit: the exact number of cherries, dramatic breakdowns, last words, next-to-last words, signs and portents—a pan had fallen from the shelf in the pantry for no reason at all; at night something had knocked on the window.

It was all so terribly far back in the past. Whether Inez's occasional abstractions were more frequent now than they used to be, whether those momentary absences of hers dated from that time, Blumentritt did not know. Sometimes her face with its translucent temples and big, thin nose was covered by a faintly oily gleam, a film of exhaustion, which she would overcome with a twitching movement of the corners of her mouth—at such times she had somewhat the look of a doctor observing a patient. That look might come when Blumentritt would ask her a question such as: "Do I have enemies?"

He asked it now. "Sometimes I really would like to know."

Then she balanced on the heel of her right foot; she enjoyed being asked questions and withholding a reply. She would stand there that way—Inez, or Issi, as he called her; he had other names for her, such as Isabella or even, at times, Gugi, but that was in the evening and not here in the shop: Frau Zergaden was not far away.

He repeated: "Tell me whether I have enemies."

"That's like telling fortunes from cards. But there isn't much you can do about the anonymous letter."

"I'm not referring to that now," he said. "But in how many directions am I insecure? Against which front should I pit forces? It's like building a dike without knowing from which side the water is going to come."

"You should never write letters to the authorities—I've told you that, time and again. If you want to be safe, don't raise your hand. That's something you should have learned from your teaching. And what's more, don't ever appeal to Heiland, unless you absolutely have to."

"It's all much more complicated than you think. To top it off, they've gone so far as to warn me against you— pardon me, I didn't mean to put that quite so bluntly. You understand what I mean—it's more or less insinuated."

"Be careful about the company you keep," she joked. "You don't have to tell me that."

"Other people are getting ahead, and you feel tied to me." She was no longed joking, but also not quite serious. "Look at Kummerbart's 'Woman Arising.' She's to be installed in the cemetery; the town is buying her. I wish I knew why."

"The town does things for its artists."

She shrugged; she knew that Kummerbart had been a terrible sculptor, but that did not interest her.

"My old white elephant. A very good offer, incidentally; I'll never have another like it. How could I refuse? I never realized its value."

"It's odd, all the same: they come to you for salt shakers and wall decorations, 'Woman Arising' or raffia shoes, and when you can supply these things, they're pleased. More than that, they have to keep on good terms with you. Whereas with us, they can order us around."

"Honestly, I don't like you to make fun of me!"

"You've misunderstood me again. I only mean to say that unfortunately my dealings are with institutions, whereas you are still on the old footing . . ."

"Nonsense." She pushed the receipt pad aside. The pencil rattled over the table, fell to the floor. Quickly she bent down to pick it up; her skirt billowed out, and as she reached a kneeling position in front of him she raised her head, looked at him with a wide-eyed smile, and said: "Too many opinions! Do you still remember how you felt about non-violence?" She was constantly reminding him that first he had sat down on the nettles with the advocates of non-violence, then plunged into the briery bush with the others who pronounced it outmoded.

"You make things too easy for yourself," he said, shaking his head, while she sprang to her feet; the doorbell had rung. "We can't do without opinions entirely."

She was interrupted by a customer. Spillner, the young museum director, entered the shop: onion head, thin red hair, nearsighted eyes raised to Inez from behind bulging glasses. Little Frau Zergaden emerged to help, and skillfully took down Spillner's order. He gave the exact measurements of a picture frame he wanted. His explanations took some time: the frame was to be bronzed, set off with black. He ignored Blumentritt, who was considering whether he should tell Inez about Kumtsiel's warning. Better not; certain truths were disturbing; perhaps the whole affair would evaporate, had only been the whim of a principal who liked to sow a little anxiety among his subordinates.

"You live chiefly in illusions," she told him, in a somewhat lower voice.

Blumentritt cautioned her with his eyes. He moved his head in the direction of Spillner. Inez's only response was to say: "That business of the letter—you know what I mean—is only an example of the trouble you stir up. Doesn't that teach you a lesson? Stop your foolishness or start selling raffia shoes."

Spillner lifted his notes close to his eyes and checked to see whether he had forgotten anything. Frau Zergaden waited, mute and inconspicuous.

We know everything about each other, Blumentritt thought. Perhaps I should tell her about Kumtsiel. It would be more honest, but possibly she will think I mean something else by it.

"Do you imagine," Inez continued, "that your letters and petitions about the apartment will have the slightest effect?" At this point Blumentritt again cautioned her with his eyes. Spillner was a municipal official, after all; he had taken over the post of Inez's father, the Archivist.

"Simply move in with me; look things squarely in the face."

"A fine joke," Blumentritt replied evasively, with a side-glance at Spillner and a rapid blinking of his eyes which signified: can't you wait until he leaves before you say such things? "Ah yes, the housing problem . . ."

"And yet so many people are running away."

Blumentritt started in alarm; he gave her an angry look and did not reply until Spillner, with a double ringing of the bell, a fifth up and a fifth down, had left the shop. "Are you mad? At least you might have a little considera-tion for me, even if you yourself don't give a damn."

"Good Lord." Frau Zergaden scurried away. Inez perched herself on the corner of the counter. "Of course they will warn you against me. They will tell you: Now look here, you've proved yourself so far, but you still haven't made a break with certain bourgeois leftovers. I'm that leftover. And yet I try so hard—I'm on excellent terms with the authorities, as you see. Let me be honest about it. I've virtually given away 'Woman Arising'; it wasn't a good offer at all. Kummerbart's heirs proposed the thing, and they're pathetically grateful to me for selling. As is the town—you'll see."

"I'm not so sure about that."

"What about you?" she asked. "They don't pay for principles. I tell myself that often, and come out pretty well."

He knew she really wanted to convince him. "This strikes me very much like a close-out sale," he said. " 'Woman Arising' is leaving the shop already, one foot forward. When are you going?"

"Never," she said. She shook her head, smiling but emphatic. "I have my house, my car, my shop, my father. He receives more from me than he earns in salary."

"I find it instructive that you've left me out of your list," Blumentritt replied. But now a new customer entered, and the conversation was at an end. Blumentritt grasped the door handle and shared with the stranger half the tinkling of the bell; the tonic note reverberated after him, and he counterpointed the slamming of the door with the impact of his walking stick on the pavement.

For some time, incidentally, Blumentritt had been looking at Frau Luja with different eyes. He caught himself mistrusting her, and wondering what lay behind her rectitude. . . . Could you possibly have written me that letter,

eh? But it's out of the question, Blumentritt; it wasn't she;
how could she do anything like that? At noon, when he
came back to his apartment for lunch, he often took out
the anonymous letter and read such sentences as: Go on
doing so and suck up to them. Musing, he opened his eyes
wide, forcing the lids as far as they would go, as though he
had to admit light to his thoughts. Whom did this abrupt
widening of the eyes remind him of? He could not recall.
He no longer had sufficient energy to fend off irritability.
And how dangerous that was. At odds with himself, he
felt threatened from two sides: by the ill will of those
who regarded him as God knows what, and by the pressure of those who were God knows what. He needed peace
and quiet in the worst way. By noon he was always exhausted, in need of some kind of refreshment. He would
wash, shave, and groom himself during the noon hour with
a care unusual in a man. He would wash his face first
with hot, then with cold water, would dry himself with a
rough towel, rubbing his face until his cheeks began to
glow a delicate red, then dab away the rest of the soap-
suds from behind and under his ears, stretch his neck—
Frau Luja was singing in the kitchen again—and dry it in
bands from top to bottom. Another soaking in hot water.
Elaborate lathering with brush and shaving soap until
his face and whiskers were covered with a layer of white
paste even in thickness. He stropped the razor and guided
it in precisely predetermined order over the bearded parts
of his face. Then he wiped away the rest of the lather. He

let his face dry by itself while he cleaned the razor and brush, then poured a stinging liquid into his hand. He distributed it evenly over his face—and now the shooting gallery opened: Bang-bang! Someone had won again. He studied himself in the mirror, let the after-shave lotion evaporate, rubbed cold cream into his burning face, then massaged his face with the ball of his thumb. He tautened and smoothed the skin, patted his cheeks and under his chin with his fingers, and reached for the talcum powder.

He had acquired these habits only after his energies began diminishing. Moreover, he had become slightly vain. But he devoted so much attention to his body chiefly because he was suffering from the dose of Luminal he took every morning. After awakening—usually very gradually —he had to take a sedative to counteract the susceptibility of his nerves, or of his brain. He was subject to a mild sort of epileptoid attack. After strong excitement, or in states of excessive fatigue, he was in danger of losing control of his limbs for seconds. The thing was trivial; perhaps he would spill the contents of a spoon while eating, or a glass would slip from his hand—no more than that. That, incidentally, was why he postponed his shaving until noon; in the morning he needed too much time to glide slowly and safely from the narcosis of sleep to the narcosis of Luminal, which then stayed with him throughout the day. Once, however, he had had one of these spells while going up the stairs, and had taken a fall. He fought against his malady; he suppressed it and did not tell anyone about it. Even Inez had found out only when she had asked him, rather shyly, although they had been together for years, why they did not get married. She should not feel tied to a sick man, he insisted, one who would do better not to beget children. Even then, he had not told her about the incident which had led to the outbreak of his sickness. He wanted to forget the cause, along with that whole murderous period, his years in the concentration camp, where one day he had been ordered: "Fall in!"

Fall in! Now leave everything aside, Blumentritt, all the feelings and little moments of forgetfulness your body permits (the brick, the brick was the result of one of those moments, Blumentritt; make your reckoning with the Lord). And forget the temporary benefaction of luke-warm, watery soup which somehow tranquilizes you. Forget, too, the time of oblivion, lying stretched out among the other sleeping men on the wooden frame you call your bed. No such thoughts are any use to you now. Now gather all your being, Blumentritt, for the whistles have sounded, the loudspeaker is announcing the roll call in the camp square, the grand Fall-in, which the inspection officer will conduct. So run, the others are already running in packs; the earth is shaking under the thomping hoofs of the herd. Thrust your body forward into the wind that blows downhill from the camp square and puffs out the men's jackets; climb the slope with all the strength of your weak knees; speed it up, throw off every preoccupation which induces vagueness; congeal into a single point, firm and insignificant and inconspicuous. That's right, for in reality only you are called; you alone are running; it is your muster, your inspection officer, your hour.

On the camp square the short banners of steam exuded from the men's lungs into the cold accumulated into smoking blocks. Commands knifed in from the sides to make order among the horde of men in stripes who kept their faces directed toward the low, oblong building which closed off the square and the camp at the top of the hill. Blumentritt, in the second row, peered between two backs which he knew so well into the narrow eyes of the oblong building, whose lids remained always closed. He lost all awareness of his surroundings; he congealed into a single point that was firm and insignificant, and comprised all his being. The commands stopped.

The inspection officer entered from the left, from the death corner, where they took those who were dead or slated to be killed. There, in that filthy corner, you parted with your life. It was no more than that: you went over there and parted with it. The crucial thing, now, was whether the chorus would be ordered to step forward. Blumentritt was experienced enough to know what took place when the chorus was used. The inspection officer looked down the blocks, whose steaming instantly decreased. Then he ordered the chorus to step forward.

At that, Blumentritt knew, even before the inspection officer called his name. Silently, the block parted around him, spewed him out into the open space between block and oblong building, while the chorus formed a semicircle to the side. Eyes dull, silent, as though he were already frozen to death, Blumentritt stood in front of the inspection officer—a tiny flame of fear only in the middle of his forehead. The inspection officer already had in hand the usual camp orders to send the prisoner Blumentritt "over the horse." But what had he done that was to be punished by flogging—twenty-five blows? Had he failed to doff his cap in time? Had he eaten at work?

The inspection officer read out the charge: Blumentritt had deliberately let a brick drop in order to smash it. He gestured toward the horse. That was why the chorus had been told to step forward. There was an old ordinance: when a prisoner went over the horse, the chorus had to step forward and sing a song, sing it in parts, for in this camp disciplinary measures were always meted out this way, so that the annoying howls of the beaten man would not be heard.

Blumentritt! Take him there, for he can't seem to walk those few steps. The horse is always too far. Now they are stripping you; the upper part of your body is pulled forward; the horse cuts into your thigh, we must say it, it must be spoken some time, one time; no one can sing it down, not the chorus, none of us, nobody. Your arms jerk down; the floggers step forward, well prepared, well nourished for their task. And the counter, a master sergeant in the SS, now takes command: Blow number one.

The chorus, clammy, agonized, steaming, barking
throats; tormented victims of a trick: the notice said,
anyone who can sing will be given a special assignment,
and then you were in for it; each time you had to step forward, each time torture your tongue, each time feel the
frozen tears behind your eyelids, the spasm in your palate.
Get going! came the shout of the inspection officer, so
that the throats cleared themselves hoarsely and slowly
laid hold of the first word. (Once again this pain in the
palate! The pain comes when you must sing against your
deepest will.) The song was always settled on beforehand.
Get going!

Blumentritt was nothing but a big flabby sphere, a ball
such as children use in play, and the blows drove into him
like nails. *Wer hat dich du schö-ner Wald.* . . . Congeal still
smaller, Blumentritt; and he thought, so they are sending
me over the horse on account of the brick, and he heard
meaningless sounds from the direction of the corner where
you lie like a shirt on the ironing board, and as the welts
blistered he bit into his tongue: Master Sergeant, Master
Ser—Master, Lord and Master, Lord—Oh my God, what
am I before You, wretched bundle of humanity that I am.

A clockwork mechanism; the odd blows from the left
(*auf-ge-baut so hoch da dro-ben*) and the even blows
from the right; gnash your teeth; spread the fingers of
your clenched hands out like wings, Blumentritt, man as

small as a billiard ball—but blows nine and eleven and twelve entered the surface of his body like hatchets. *Wohl den Mei-ster will ich lo-ben, so lang noch*—spit out your tongue, Blumentritt—*will ich lo-ben*—jaws flapped in the gusts from the lungs which squeezed the song out of their throats—*so lang noch mein' Stimm' erschallt.*

In between, what had happened. In between, between this and—scream, Blumentritt—the next blow, what had happened. Why are you shaking so, you dog Blumentritt? That's how it had begun. Why do you insult the others by your shaking? Don't shake like that, the squad leader at the building site had said; come, stand on this railroad track here; that will quiet you down, you dog Blumentritt, good God, man. And as Blumentritt (now, a day later, shrunk to a speck under the blows, a congealed node of humanity embedded in a fiery, knotted mass of pain)—as Blumentritt saved his life by carrying out the order and trying to stand immobile on the railroad track, suppressing his shaking and swaying, and as the icy pain stiffened and thinned his body, the squad leader said simply: There, now pick up a brick. That always helps. Then you'll feel better; that gives you energy, exercise, keeps you strong and healthy. Weight warms, and the shaking will pass too, dog Blumentritt, good God, man. And (if his life were worth anything to him) he had to get a brick, for he did not dare disobey the order. He lifted it from the ground with his numbed, frozen hands and pressed his arms together, since he wasn't certain that his fingers were gripping it. Then he stood up on the rail again. But his arms gave way, and as he leaned forward, wanting to cup his hands under the brick, a club struck him in the back, for no order had been given to bend forward on the rail. He slipped off, but immediately leaped back, his body tilted sideways as though he wanted to lay his head to rest on the rail forever, for all eternity. And as he did so, the brick slipped from his stiff, nerveless hands and broke. That was his crime.

Now, as Blumentritt's screams burst forth and blood sprayed from his lips as he bit them in his pain, the master sergeant conducted the whole performance. His glance swept over the mute blocks of prisoners and he urged the chorus on by shaking his fist at them: *Le-be wohl, le-be wohl, du schöner Wald.* The master sergeant checked Blumentritt's position on the horse and complained that some of his clothing had worked up over the red arcs incised by the lashes; and while the spasmodic mouths in semicircle barked: *Hast du treu uns auf-er-zogen,* he gave the beat to floggers, first right, then left, right, left, and into the whistling swish of the lashes as they descended cut the howl of Blumentritt's tongue, against his will; he summoned up all his will; the will—*from-mer Sa-gen Auf-enthalt*—clenched itself again, but capitulated. The twenty-second blow: *Was wir still gelobt im Wald*—scream, Blumentritt—*wol-lens draussen ehrlich halten*—go on, scream, scream, let them strain their lungs even more so that you don't have to hear your own screams, even if their palates split with the pain; your screams are held in the screech of their voices! *Ewig blei-ben treu die Al-ten.* Twenty-third blow, last stanza, Blumentritt; you're dying; ah, to what a point have you congealed that the fires burn you so? How deep? You are burning up, the lava layer of pain is too thick—*deutsch Panier, das rauschend wallt*—twenty-fourth blow, one more, they are punctilious, no arbitrary punishments here, not a blow too many, the master sergeant has counted each one, turns his eyes away from the horribly mangled lump in front of him, prefers to shake his fist at the others, spurring on their song, so that no other sound will be audible before the end, louder, still louder: *Le-be wohl!* Last bloody slash across the hip. *Schirm dich Gott, du deutscher Wald.* Twenty-fifth blow, your thoughts are dying, Blumentritt, you've had it—but that is only the dissolution of the nucleus into which you congealed. You're going to live, you dog Blumentritt, good God, man.

He had been flogged; that was the origin of his weakness. He could keep the illness in check if he used tablets regularly to tranquilize his brain, which caused these momentary slips. But that made him susceptible to fatigue; the drug made his body flabby, and in order to conserve his remaining energies he had to tend his body with unusual care. This constant struggle between illness and self-preservation, limpness and liveliness, was gradually painting dark shadows in the folds which scored his face from top to bottom. A glance in the mirror showed him that.

His pale tan complexion was lighter from the cheeks up to the forehead. His hair hung down over his brow and fell in layers over his ears; it was as dark as his eyes, which were sunk deep in their sockets; curiously small, sometimes holding a glow like a fading spark. The look in them, astonishment and alienation, as if he might burst into unpremeditated laughter, kept people at a distance. No one ever directly molested him; people kept out of his way and were generally polite and obliging, except in letters; and even receiving nasty letters was a new experience for him.

Stripped to the waist, he finished his toilette. He was sturdily built, as he now noted in the mirror once again, and with satisfaction. He had broad shoulders and the base of his neck was unusually stocky. He had become so accustomed to his stiff leg that it no longer bothered him at all. It had been injured one day in camp when, detailed to prove his fitness, he had been clearing out the concrete halls of a shattered munitions plant. There had been an explosion, he had come to in the hospital, and from there had been discharged. Thereafter his knee joint was out of commission. To that stiff leg he owed his freedom, perhaps his survival. Since it hampered him only slightly, he had preferred not to have an operation; on certain occasions it gave him a pretext for limping along in the rear, or not going along at all. Nothing to be unhappy about. He even felt a certain contentment and snugness when, having finished his toilette, he stretched his leg out on a chair, rested a pile of notebooks on his thigh, and began correcting them.

Windstorms were rare here. (The dead man swayed perpetually outside his window.) This storm whirled up the dust. It was mingled with rain, delicate streaks and strings of rain which the wind whirled in circles around the lamp post. (Dead men do not age.) In the Fish Market the shooting gallery, carousel, and wheel of fortune booths stood with mouths opened to empty space, swallowing rain. The weekly market ended at noon; the peddlers took down their stands. Wooden sawhorses stood about everywhere. As soon as the clouds cast a scurrying shadow over the square (or in spring, when the trees stretched out their earliest greenery and the leaves, dark flecks against the sky, tumbled about), he would see the hanged man again as he had that first time.

The wind toyed with the remnants of the morning's market, scraps of newspaper flew though the air, thump of wood as counters were taken apart, boards thrown onto wagons. Blumentritt thought of Inez, how much he needed her. In these sagging moments, wearinesses, he could not pull himself together quickly; the steady use of Luminal had shattered his self-control. This was not the time for correcting notebooks and reading; his body, recurrently a nuisance, distracted him, brought the notion of another body, Inez on his knees, or in front of him, beside him, stooping over him; she moved her shoulders inside her dress, something visible, naked touched him, touch, she smelled of fresh rain water and these wearinesses, this warmth rain down drizzle against the panes her shoulder her hand a breath against his mouth, wind whistling outside, why was she running about in the rain, why was she negotiating with authorities over purchase prices or delivery contracts instead of being here? He hunched over the desk, his eyes narrowing, lips compressed; he propped his arms on the desk top. Outside, pale spirals whirled around the lamp post; he glanced briefly at it and remembered: how she glided down beside him suddenly her left arm under his neck remembered the sound of the smell of a movement of startled perception—her right hand dangled down visibility she should be but why isn't she here always these wearinesses and the warmth and the numbness in every limb sometimes impossible to think of anything else. (This wind.) And then he gave a sudden slide, a lurch, his hand flashed in front of his face, what was that, his arm fell from the tabletop, he awoke, was wide awake. It was a noise, but nothing close by, a gentle, faraway crash; it struck and almost stunned him. He thought it must be his nerves, and closed his eyes, but nothing changed; it had nothing to do with his nerves, nor had it been a dream; he was wide awake, and in the next breath he knew what it was. The noise came from outside, a metallic clang followed by the tinkle of breaking glass.

Blumentritt jumped up and went to the window. Then he saw it: the wind had broken the lamp post in two. Only the lower half of the pole was standing. He could imagine how it had happened: rust at the slenderest part of the pole, long years of rust, decades when it ate away at the iron, and the wind shaking the pole time and again, the metal growing tired, and then this storm: the lamp post vibrating back and forth, a crack, a small gouge, metal splintering off, the post bending, the upper half crashing down. That was how it must have happened. The two-tined fork had struck exactly on the parking place at the edge of the square; a few oldish vehicles, most of them two-cycle engines, stood there. And, Blumentritt recognized it, Inez's car also stood there, her Hanomag. One of the arms of the lamp post had smashed in the roof; the windshield was shattered. The big baby-bottle lamps (how huge those shades were) lay in the middle of the street, broken off by the impact. Now the first pedestrians came along and with their feet pushed the lamps to the curb. Metal scraped over asphalt.

No one had been hurt. Blumentritt could not suppress a sudden surge of malicious delight that this particular car had been struck. He did not wish Inez the vexation, but she ought to learn the lesson; she always took everything too lightly and made fun of him when he suffered from the banalities of daily life, from vexations of just this kind. Something was always hitting him, aiming directly at him. (You attract it, she said, you draw it to you.) Should he go down now and mingle with the curious crowd who were standing around the car? Inez was nowhere in sight. He asked Frau Luja to bring him his lunch. She had heard about the accident and had been down to the street twice. She knew exactly where someone had been standing when the lamp post broke, who had been standing right there only shortly before, where the big lamps with their sheet-metal shades had struck, so that it was a providence that . . . She recollected similar cases: a big fire in the castle many, many years ago; a roof beam fell just where some-one had been standing only a short while before—who had it been? at the foot of a ladder incidentally a friend of her husband's, a distant relative, not to speak of her hus-band, who had so often been miraculously, she remem-bered so many cases, miraculously saved, and then in the thirties when there was that terrible railroad accident in Grossheringen on Christmas Eve—he hadn't wanted to leave that day and had almost missed the seven o'clock train and then at the last moment he'd jumped aboard (which he never used to do; she'd always warned him about jumping aboard a moving train) and it had to be just that train and on Christmas Eve into the bargain. Tears choked her voice. It was all Providence. Frau Luja stepped to the window behind Blumentritt's back and clapped her hands noisily: just imagine if something happened now! She was so overwrought that in going out she forgot how hard the door opened and so she ran her stomach and tightly-laced bosom against the door panel; for a moment her face hovered rigidly in front of the wood until a second assault opened the door.

During the afternoon Blumentritt went to the window several times to see what was being done with the battered car. But there was no activity around it, no sign of Inez; she abided by their strict agreement not to call on him in his apartment, and toward evening, when he looked out again after some interval, the car had disappeared.

Blumentritt's satisfaction that the lamp post, the two-armed gallows, no longer existed, remained with him. That specter had existed long enough; it dated back to the days of the Kaiser. Uhlans had filed beneath it; old residents of Schochern still had yellowed post cards showing such parades. Later there had been the demonstrations of a political party seeking power, and counterdemonstrations, fifes competing with bugles, shaken fists and raised hands. It had always ended in a brawl. Rubber-truncheon salad when the police intervened; rubber-truncheon salad, people in Schochern called it. And then one day all that was over, thereafter nothing but goosestepping columns, blare of brass; and then that too ceased and instead came mass meetings, speeches, speeches, Rosa Luxembourg and Karl Liebknecht, down with, forward to, *da steht ein Mann*, *ein Mann, so fest wie eine Eiche, vielleicht sind wir schon morgen eine Leiche,* carnival in the dark, enough, over and done with, the gallows gone. Blumentritt was happy.

That very evening he went to see Inez in the house on Crooked Hill. He had his own key, but did not need to take it from his pocket; she was expecting him. He had thought she would rant a bit at what had happened to her car (though ranting was scarcely her style; when she did, she sounded like a nun trying to curse). But she did not rant at all; she seemed to accept the whole thing with philosophy. She only dropped into a chair and said that of course she would *not* go to the Town Hall and make a fuss, she would *never* do that; she would send in a report of the damage and wait politely. "Forget the loss. If you go there, you're done for."

"And suppose you have trouble? Suppose they do not replace the car?" he asked.

She did not take him up on that. "One has to handle these situations by instinct. I've had experience."

"Sometimes you strike me as almost abnormal," he said. The conversation was lame from the start. He stared at the figures in the carpet.

She replied in one of her standard phrases, which sounded on her lips like irony directed at herself: "Women do see everything differently, you know!" She crossed her legs. "That's nothing you could understand."

"Perhaps."

"But it isn't your fault. Men are usually dense. You all

76)

have too many principles. Either you batter down the wall with your heads, or you kill yourselves in the process."

"Something else is involved," he said. "It's a feeling for a natural order of things, a kind of equilibrium, which may be particularly strong in nervous personalities. To put it another way: paradox kills us; we want to restore the balance, one way or the other. I must tell you about something in my childhood, something that probably never happens to a girl. As a child, I don't know how old I was, but it was after I was going to school—as a child, when I spun myself around twice in a room, I felt I absolutely had to spin around an equal number of times to the left. It was an irresistible compulsion. Does that mean anything to you? Perhaps there are better examples. Everyone has experienced the same thing in different ways. And yet I was not given to brooding; I wasn't a shy and unworldly child. But, aside from sheer nervousness, there was a feeling for balance in that, or to translate it into moral terms: a sense that proper equilibrium must be restored."

"Such disturbances occur in puberty," Inez replied.

He had no comment to make on that subject. She liked to talk about the age which she called puberty, about her schoolgirl years. It drew her mind away from her troubles —no, that was the wrong phrase—rather, it drew her mind to herself. They both had the clearest memories of those years, memories that were markedly physical. All excitements, sweet anxieties, lassitudes, had been experi-

(77

enced for the first time: she on a school bench in a thin, bright dress; he all expectation, pursuer; and any thought of those years would instantly transport them into a condition in which every harmless word such as stocking, bedroom, perfume, rubber, position had an erotic connotation. He sometimes suspected that she purposely gave the conversation this particular turn, so that he would desire her, and then, as though she had had nothing of the sort in mind, would come the innocently astonished widening of her eyes. And when he embraced her, he saw, just as he touched her shoulder with a first clumsy movement, the way she raised her arm a little unsteadily and (Good Lord, no one could dissimulate so skillfully) remained motionless with open mouth, as though she had never imagined that he would want that of her now; and he would again decide that she had had no ulterior purpose and would tell himself: after all, she is a child, and not even a clever one.

One evening Blumentritt had a visitor. The evening had begun with no hint of anything unusual. Blumentritt was sitting by the floor lamp, leafing through a textbook, something he seldom got to, when the ringing of the doorbell surprised him. He was not often disturbed at night— never by Inez, out of consideration for Frau Luja, who had her opinions about their relationship. Ordinarily his only visitors were pupils, and they came by day. So who could be ringing? He anticipated Frau Luja and went to the hall door. Through the frosted glass the outline of a tall figure showed in the dusky stairwell. When he opened the door, he confronted a man whom he did not immediately recognize, although his face was well-known to him. He admitted his visitor, led him into his room, and only then, in the light of the floor lamp, did he realize that it was Archivist Meiran, Inez's father. Meiran—educated natives of the town sometimes spelled the name Majoran (marjoram) by mistake, because the herb was locally pronounced *Meiran*. Meiran kept a dachshund which he called Majoran.

Meiran was no longer in the municipal employ. Presumably he had long ago passed the age limit. In his best years he had acquired a certain prestige from a learned study of the basic forms of the German household. Unfortunately he had been a Freemason, and this fact rather suddenly put a stop to his career one day. He lived through the Third Reich, keeping himself tolerably busy as a private scholar, undertaking excavations, collecting art treasures, which would later prove useful to his daughter, storing up knowledge, and waiting for his hour to come. At last, after the end of the war, he was offered a public post; he replaced as municipal archivist a man who had compromised himself by writing a pamphlet on the swastika as a decorative emblem, the disseminator of aphorisms and maxims, Paul Josua Keil.

Meiran was wearing a green corduroy jacket so old and worn as to be almost gray. Blumentritt thought he recalled that the archivist had worn a green corduroy jacket as far back as he could remember—if not this jacket, then a predecessor which resembled it to a hair in color, and ridge for ridge. The man stood, shoulders drooping, green and faded, in the room. Blumentritt drew up the desk chair for himself and invited his visitor to sit in the upholstered armchair, the only one in the room. Now the light of the floor lamp fell upon Meiran's face.

That face had something harrowed about it, a kind of mummified mimicry, a rapid fire of moving images, as if seen under a celluloid filter. The nose was blunted at its bridge and sloped down into the general pallor of the face, becoming cold and waxen. The brow bulged above it. The area that surrounded the eyes, which seemed to enlarge itself when he spoke and grew excitable, was also white and lifeless; it looked rather like a ring around the moon. The corners of his mouth twitched in response to every emotion; in the course of time two folds had formed there, running downward and away from the lips. When he prepared to say something important and wrung his hands, when his forehead worked and his eyebrows began to dance, arching up into his brow and forming two undulations, when he tilted his head back and pressed his chin against his throat—the restiveness of his face became controlled and was summed up by the sign language of his eyes.

"Perhaps you will resent this interference," he began in a choked voice. "In that case I should not have come to see you. Very well. You know my daughter, know her well, and that encourages me. Only I wouldn't want you to tell her that I came to see you—please do not. I've come on account of my daughter, but what will I accomplish?" he said, closing his eyes and then opening them abruptly once more. His face expressed utter perplexity. Then the furrows suddenly disappeared from his brow, his eyes dropped shut again—there was an infinite number of variations. Between the closing and opening of his eyes there was still a third stage: when he raised his eyebrows but let his eyelids shutter the shifted pupils, which glimmered through the narrow crack. Along with these facial spasms he threw his entire head back; it was a state of visible strain, followed immediately by relaxation—a spectacle Blumentritt watched with fascination, without breaking in with any word of his own.

"Can one," Meiran continued, "can one accordingly expect you to exert any influence upon my daughter? Or would that be asking too much?"

Blumentritt became embarrassed; he propped his elbows on his knees and pressed the tips of his fingers so tightly together that all the blood receded from them. "That depends."

"It is all a question of clarity," Meiran said, "which I am determined to obtain. My daughter tells me nothing; we're not on bad terms, but she tells me nothing. You,

Herr Blumentritt, associate with her; I know that, even approve it—although I have no call to approve or disapprove. Accordingly, this association might, of course, tie Inez down, weaken her resolution."

"What makes you say that?"

"I don't understand what is in my daughter's mind. As long as Keil was living, I visited her home sometimes; now I scarcely ever do. She no longer likes me to, has no use for me; I also don't know the direction in which she is steering the business. Toward participation by the state? That would be the end. Or what she needs a free hand for. She is making compromises, is committing, is committing an . . ." Large, waxy-pale spots around his eyes contracted, but he could not bring out the word. "Well then, you shouldn't hold Inez here!" he said at last.

"I haven't any such desire—I'm completely surprised— I don't influence her in the least!" Blumentritt replied. "And if she had the intention to flee—but she has no such intention . . ."

"You should convince her to!" Meiran demanded. Then he turned away in sudden embarrassment, as though frightened by his own lack of caution.

"But really!" Blumentritt struggled for words. "How can you possibly want Inez to leave you?"

There was a pause. "I would rather be separated from her," Meiran answered at last, "and at least feel that one of us has reached the other shore."

"That is"—Blumentritt hesitated—"that is hard, bitter, inhuman. How can you think such thoughts!"

"Good Lord!" Meiran said.

"No, I don't understand you," Blumentritt continued. "Inez isn't suffering; she runs the shop, has a car—though not at the moment—all right, but she has a house, everything she needs, and still you wish . . ."

"I see you cannot follow my reasoning. Very well. And what about the story with Keil? Granted, that was long ago. You refuse to understand. Suppose she is well off? What difference does that make? This is precisely the best time. The strange thing is: why isn't she having any difficulties with Heiland? Why has he ordered 'Woman Arising' from her? Why is this dangerous neighbor behaving in so ostentatiously quiet a manner? That's what has you fooled. That's it."

"I can well understand," Blumentritt said, "that since the incident with your son-in-law you . . ." At that moment the light went out; they could no longer see one another. Should he grope his way into the bedroom and bring the candle which he always had ready for such emergencies? Perhaps the outage would not last long, or else Frau Luja would come. "I understand that you don't think well of Heiland, but your distrust of Inez is unjustified."

"No," Meiran replied firmly, ignoring the darkness. Now Blumentritt could not even tell whether he was jiggling his eyebrows as he talked. "No, no, it looks very

much as if she has bought Heiland's forebearance, and that
is . . ."

Once again he failed to bring out the treacherous word.
Blumentritt wondered whether he ought to continue the
conversation at all. What did the man want of him? Could
he possibly have written the anonymous letter? He spoke,
but feared that his words, with an explanatory, propitiat-
ing gesture now invisible, would only increase the misunderstanding between them. "Perhaps you are unjust.
Everyone must make certain compromises, must adapt
himself, in order to survive. Experience teaches that."

"You don't know what Heiland did," Meiran insisted.
"Or else you have forgotten."

"All right. But we are all only human. Your daughter
Inez too. You think about her a great deal, brood, assume
the worst, when her life may only be taking a different
course, one strange to you."

"Life," Meiran replied, still undisturbed by the dark. "I
know all about that. I've not been retired for so very long.
Granted, I haven't resigned myself, or put an end to it all,
like Keil. I still have a measure of ambition, at least for my
daughter. We old men are tenacious. We even know how
to wait."

"What for?" Blumentritt asked; but he instantly felt
ashamed of the ruthlessness of his question, and added:
"Weren't you pensioned? You say that you still have
ambitions for your daughter; but I detect a good deal of
personal disillusionment in your words."

The response was laughter, which disturbed him.

"Disillusionment!" Meiran exclaimed after a while. "Have you ever heard of the vault in the castle?"

"Of course." Blumentritt kept hoping that the light would come back on; but Meiran launched into his story, as though he wanted to take advantage of the darkness.

"As you know, the last counts of Schochern are buried in that vault. The tombs of these noblemen were thrown open to the public, I don't know when. Long ago, at any rate. Toward the end of the war someone must have opened the sarcophagi; everything was in total confusion in those days. The same was true for the vault; the sarcophagi were open and the bones were knocking all over the place. A teacher who used to take his pupils to see the vault even allowed them to use the bones as bowling pins. How long is this light going to be out? Conditions changed, of course, when I took over the archives and along with them the responsibility for the vault."

Blumentritt had given up hope that Frau Luja would come in. But he also did not dare get up and go for the candle. Something compelled him to listen with closest attention, and as he listened he observed that Meiran had a very high, chanting voice which he fed by breath squeezed out of his chest.

"It was a difficult task for me; you can well believe that. What was I to do? Everything was a mess. I made a complaint about the condition of the vault—to this day I have the carbon copy of my memorandum—but nothing was done. And so I attended to it myself, at least sealed up the vault again. And one day a commission came along, asked why I was not admitting anyone, inspected everything, and vanished. Weeks passed—what am I saying, months. Then suddenly came the order that I was not to keep the vault closed but to put it into decent condition; things could not be allowed to go as they had been going; I was to put the sarcophagi in order and repair all traces of previous neglect. The reason given was that the last count had fought a bitter struggle against the Electoral Prince, who had wanted to swallow up the county of Schochern. The count, the argument went, had thus, in a period of despotic absolutism, ranged himself on the side of the rising city states. A fine reason, isn't it?"

"Of course." Blumentritt had inhibitions about speaking out into the darkness. "What more could you have wanted —your memorandum was a success. You had been justified, whether or not the count was a good man."

"To be frank, I didn't care about that."

"I can well understand you."

"But how foolish!" Meiran laughed. "How foolish! Don't you foresee the sequel? How can anyone count on such justifications? By the next mail—the next mail, mind you, the District Commission for the Care of Monuments revoked its orders to restore the vault."

"Probably a mistake . . ."

"Not on your life," Meiran cried triumphantly. "No mistake at all. Or would you like to call it a mistake that every existing state—including this one—has rediscovered nationalism for itself? Nothing, my friend, is too old and worn out not to be dusted off and trotted out again! Now listen closely: What the count had done, his rebellion against the Electoral Prince, was—seen in the proper light —a simple case of particularism, an attempt to perpetuate the system of small states. Do you follow the reasoning? But the nation state represents progress; therefore not a cent must be wasted on the vault. Consequently, when I published a short article in a local history journal, and announced that the vault was open for interested visitors, I received a bristling letter."

Meiran paused, evidently to summon back to mind the contents of the letter. "The documents are all still available; a pity I don't have the copies with me; they'd help me straighten out the order of events. Because it's a longish story, you understand. Though at the moment we couldn't read the documents anyhow." Blumentritt heard his laughter. "So then I received a letter criticizing my conduct. Where the devil is the light? The vault must be closed immediately; in fact, the entrance from the castle must be cemented up. By this time I'd given up protesting against these decrees, since I had no arguments. After all, I've never been a particularist." Meiran laughed again.

"But you weren't dismissed on that account, were you?" Blumentritt asked. He was beginning to feel cooped up in the room, whose walls seemed suddenly to have closed in.

"Dismissed? It's a longish story, as I said. Are you interested?"

"Very much so," Blumentritt assured him, although he could not imagine that the vault had been opened again.

"Came the anniversary of Balthasar Kempff. Very well, the composer Kempff, seventeenth century, an early master of the motet. He had worked for a considerable time at the court of the count in question."

"What has Balthasar Kempff to do with it?"

"I'm going to explain that. In Schochern, as everywhere else, we had a festival week. You know the sort of thing. Concerts were given, speeches made, memorial celebrations held. So-and-so gets up and says this and that and we put up with it and think it a treat if one of the speakers turns out to be a real student of the subject, a scholar, a specialist. Now there happens to be a West German scholar who has written an authoritative book on Kempff. He was invited, and came. Naturally we were all eager to hear that particular talk, on the chance we would really learn something. And sure enough, our guest speaker elaborated on the relations, the very pleasant relations between the composer and the young count. It was an easygoing relationship, a real friendship, in fact. Kempff had composed a number of important works in Schochern and had dedicated them to the count. Our speaker had therefore decided—this was the note on which he ended his talk, I noted the words carefully—he had decided 'to take advantage of this opportunity' to pay tribute to the

count by laying a wreath on his grave, or on his sarcoph-
agus, in his vault . . ."

At this point Meiran made an artful pause. Blumentritt
heard breathing; it was his own.

"Naturally a great effort was made to get rid of this
inconvenient muddlehead of a scholar as quickly as possible. Good Lord, suppose he actually visited that vault!
They managed to embroil him in receptions, dinners,
sightseeing tours; they saw to it that there simply wasn't
an hour to spare, not a single opportunity for laying that
wreath. The moment he rose from the table, delegations
of young people surrounded him; if he suggested going
up to the castle, the Mayor was on the spot with the keys
to the city. And then suddenly he was gone; his time had
run out and he had to return home. But I could guess what
would follow, what an uproar this innocent and simple-
hearted man would leave behind. Naturally the vault had
to be unsealed again! There had been representatives of
some of the highest agencies at the ceremonies, and these
people had observed the game of hide-and-seek with the
eminent musicologist. That sort of thing wouldn't do,
must never happen again. And so, always ready to obey
the will of my superiors and not being born yesterday, I
sent for the masons and the restorers. To tell the truth, I
had a hard time fitting all these expenses into the city's
budget. That wasn't my concern, of course, but it earned
me the enmity of a man you know—Heiland."

Blumentritt remained silent. Unable to punctuate

the darkness, he let himself fall under the spell of the voice.

"You ought to hear that letter," Meiran continued, "that magnificent letter extolling the count for reviving the music and culture of his devastated county after the Thirty Years' War. The vault must be opened. So far so good. A year passed." He paused to dramatize the passage of time. "Then came the collectivization of agriculture. A congress of farmers took place in Schochern—perhaps you remember. It was a time of great changes in the rural areas, and a big point was made of the former serfdom of the peasants. How was it phrased? Oh yes: 'In the days of the count, the peasants had to deliver the fruits of their bitter toil to their overlord. They who had groaned most under the burdens of the war now bled for the exploiters.' That was the wording of one resolution. Where the devil is the light? 'But they, the feudal lords, caroused and feasted in their castles. And to this day a veritable cult is made of them at the castle in Schochern! A shortsighted administration has allowed the ruling classes of those times to be glorified and an inadequate picture of the true conditions of the period to be presented in the museum. We demand: Fresh air in the robbers' lair!' Heiland was behind that resolution. Of course it's true that the counts caroused and whored like pigs—forgive the expression. But was that my fault? Was that newspaper article necessary?"

Blumentritt pressed his hands against his knees. He

could not even see the outlines of Meiran's head. "Well
—what did you do then?"

"I closed the vault. As ordered. Only—hold on a moment. Everything went on deteriorating, as desired. I received no more funds to improve matters. No funds, mind
you, for now . . ."

At last the electric current came back; the floor lamp
glowed, flickered reddishly for a moment, and then resumed its normal brightness. Meiran had closed his eyes.
"Mind what I say: no more funds . . ."

"Why did you need funds? You were relieved of all
responsibility for maintenance."

Blumentritt felt stronger since the light was on again;
it was like a rescue.

"Why did I need funds?" Meiran echoed him. "A curator thinks differently, my friend."

The absurd succession of events was gradually beginning to plague Blumentritt like an unlocalizable pain which
keeps moving from one spot of the body to another.
This must end some time!

"A curator sees these things in a different light," Meiran
assured him, "especially when the government suddenly
remembers its so-called cultural heritage, under which
heading castles and monuments belong. The upshot of it
all was this: the city all too readily certified that nothing
was being done for the care of its historic sites. I was discharged, relieved of my post, for neglecting my duty to
look after such cultural monuments. Why else? Oddly

enough, I don't even know precisely what the reason was. In any case, it was all a pretext to deprive me of my just pension. The pension I receive today is ridiculous. But at least I do have the consolation that the vault is no longer my worry, but my successor's—the idiot."

"I'll take a look at it some time," Blumentritt said, exhausted.

"That will scarcely be possible. At some time or other it was quietly closed again. I can't even tell you when."

Meiran rose, and his over-mobile face relaxed. "I don't know whether all this means anything to you. I must apologize for having taken so much of your time. But believe me: no one is immune; one falls into the net all too easily." Meiran shook himself as if he were cold. The sleeves of his corduroy jacket scuffed over the ridges of the front; he said goodbye. Blumentritt saw him to the door. There Meiran said: "When I say that, I am thinking of my daughter. Do you understand me? When all that is involved, what does an art shop matter, I ask you?"

When Blumentritt was alone again, he placed the book he had been reading (*Fundamental Types of Germanic Agrarian Settlements*, edited for schools) back on the shelf. He looked out on the remains of the lamp post, the dimly visible iron stump. Once again he thought of Heiland.

What should one do? Always more, always new charges, but where was the tribunal before whom to present them?

·   ·   ·

The workmen came in the morning. He heard the commotion in the square; they unloaded apparatus from the truck and set up a mechanical ladder. Were they going to remove the remainder of the lamp post? The truck disgorged not only tools, but pieces of iron, steel collars, and rope for a windlass. The welders called loudly for fire, were lifted by the ladder, were provided with flame, and went to work. Blumentritt kept his eyes fixed on the cutting tools; he wanted to see the shaft glow red-hot and split. But this sight was not granted him, for the jagged broken end was merely smoothed. No work of destruction began that way. The section of the lamp post which lay on the ground was only neatly trimmed, not carried away. It was fitted into . . .

Now the municipal radio: *Ein Mann wie eine Eiche!* And Blumentritt thought: what could he do about it? Go to Heiland? He had only to cross one street and then another; it was no further to the Town Hall. (*Vielleicht sind wir schon morgen eine Leiche*—maybe we'll be corpses tomorrow, the loudspeaker promised.) Could anyone who did not have that lamp post standing before his own window feel as he did? How could he convey his viewpoint?

But he left the house. The impression was still fresh in his mind: it would be a senseless waste of money to preserve that thing like a monument, as a relic of the gloomy past. Yes, that was the way he would put it to Heiland! Armed, under the immediate impetus of this moment, he

(93

would confront the authorities and state his honest opinion; after all, there wasn't any law against that, was there? As yet.

The way to Heiland led through three anterooms, and in the second of them sat little Frau Zergaden. You here, Blumentritt almost asked; what does this mean? But he remained silent. Nothing surprised him any more; he no longer regarded anything as fantastic and did not want to waste any time. The salary was better here; she had to move up. Fair enough, he thought, that's reasonable. She looked around to see whether the doors to the adjoining rooms were closed. "Frau Keil was not allowed to pay me any more, so we parted on good terms," she said.

"Fair enough. Please announce me to the mayor."

"That isn't my function; I'll pass you on."

She let him precede her; at his back he felt the suction of her eyes. In the third room he was received by a matronly woman in a violet dress. "Have you an appointment?" she asked.

"No," he replied. "There was no time for me to make one."

The secretary hunched her head between her shoulders; her violet-clad bosom dipped to the desk. "And what do you want to see the mayor about?"

"Please don't make a fuss, just announce me." Blumentritt gave his name. The secretary vanished and returned, evidently surprised that the name was really enough.

Heiland received him with clumsy superiority—a man

playing the part of someone sitting at his desk. His face lit up; he straightened up his back to simulate dignity. To each side of his rows of yellow teeth, through which he strenuously drew short, stertorous breaths, the folds around his mouth crooked in a meager smile. Blumentritt noted the grooves on the mayor's chin and cheeks. For a moment Heiland removed his glasses and directed his small, moist bird's eyes at his visitor. Without the glasses, Heiland's face showed nervous strain barely under control, like a field of smoothed-down rubble; when he replaced them, there remained only the costly victory of an idea.

"Good you've come!" His voice had a restrained quiver; his hands brushed with some pride over the desk top, heaped with documents, newspapers, and sheets of memo pads.

Blumentritt took a swift view of his surroundings. Between the yellow file cases hung framed photographs. One wall was empty, its wallpaper showed a somewhat lighter rectangle; and behind Heiland's back was suspended the life-size head of a man, framed behind glass. He was the promoter of sports, of youth, of hiking, of heavy industry, agriculture, and literature; he looked over Heiland's shoulder and down upon the visitor with an austere smile.

Blumentritt wanted to plunge right in and, to illustrate the reason for his visit, lead Heiland to look out the window. But there was nothing there; the window did not face the front of the Fish Market; it gave on a courtyard or side street. Moreover, noise did not penetrate into this room. A stagnant stillness prevailed, punctuated only by the dripping, creaking, and knocking of the steam heat. Before Blumentritt had quite gathered himself together to speak, Heiland began.

"No doubt you are wondering why the permit for the printing has taken so long to come through, and wanted to see about the matter yourself," he said. "That is good, that is quite right. It might have slipped my mind entirely. I was going to ask you whether you still insist on having it. In the pressure of business I might not have got around to writing you. Well?"

"I don't quite understand," Blumentritt replied, thrown completely off course. What had that been about? He did not recall having requested any such thing. "Permission to print? You may be thinking of someone else. I have never asked you for anything of the sort and have come for an entirely different reason, something much more pressing and obvious."

"Hold on, hold on, we'll come back to it." Heiland raised his hand gently in a restraining gesture and bowed his head, staving off any dislocation of his agenda. "Let's take it slowly; no doubt you are concerned about"—he leaned back somewhat, as if to convince himself from a greater distance of the correctness of his assertion—"about a text you authored? Something written? Something you wanted to have printed?"

Now Blumentritt understood, although he did not yet see how the matter had come to Heiland. He had gone to a printer, an old acquaintance, and commissioned a small printing job—so far, so good. Possibly the printer needed a license number, such as was mandatory for every postal card, every letterhead, and every marriage announcement, and possibly that was the reason it had taken so long (actually, Blumentritt had scarcely given the matter any thought). But the printing shop always took care of that end of it; it was not something you bothered about yourself, and the printer had never even mentioned the matter. What had it to do with Heiland?

"How has the whole thing come to you? It's an altogether insignificant matter."

"It may seem so to you," Heiland explained. "But it is not so simple. The head of the department did not know what to do with your stuff, since he usually deals only with engagement cards and concert programs. And, after all, someone has to pass on the text, you know! You can understand that. Consequently, it was sent on to me. Here"—he began rummaging in his desk drawer—"here, I have it now. There must be some copies here too." He closed the desk drawer and took a batch of files from a slotted cabinet on the right of the desk. Quickly, he found what he was looking for: carefully prepared copies on official paper, with attached memoranda and filing slips— quite a procedure. Blumentritt was gradually beginning to recall the sentences he had written, which must be on

(97

these copies; he reconstructed them in his mind and went over them. A description of a village street, whirling dust from vehicles, a puddle by the roadside, a pregnant woman in front of a house, touched by the crimson glow of a setting sun. Those were his impressions of a moment with Inez. Or the scene by the pond: recollection of an experience with a girl, croaking frogs. Blumentritt leaned forward toward the desk, as though he would more easily discover how these sketches had landed here.

"So you wanted to have these things printed," Heiland studied the copy. "And for whom? For the public, of course; otherwise people do not have things printed. In thus turning to . . ."

"But that's nonsense," Blumentritt blurted out. "I wanted to give copies to friends, that's all."

"All the same, the material will reach readers—say ten, or fifty, or one. The number does not matter."

"But I didn't mean to sell it to anyone! It's something altogether unimportant, like a pen sketch or a letter; something purely private, don't you see? I'm not harming anyone by printing it."

"But to whom is it useful? That is the question we must ask. If we give out a permit to print . . ."

Blumentritt sighed. He leaned back, raised his stiff leg from the floor so that it rested on the edge of his chair, and looked across the desk, up at the wall (the eyes of the man in the portrait on the wall met his), and then into Heiland's face. He looked searchingly, helplessly, despairingly. He felt unprepared to go into all these questions; he had wanted to vent his anger by some kind of outburst, even if a restrained one—and now came this. An emotional eruption, once checked and delayed, was virtually robbed of all effect. With each passing minute his call on Heiland was losing more and more meaning, value, and prospect of success; he could see that the cause, for whose sake alone he had ventured this visit, was already lost. The awareness of that numbed him, brought him to the verge of physical pain. His throat and the back of his neck grew hot; he turned and twisted his neck inside his shirt collar, thrust his forefinger under his collar, and at last groaned: "But please . . . !"

"Yes," Heiland went on, undeterred, "you see we must ask ourselves: whom do you hope to serve by printing such a thing. You do not serve our people. Our people . . ." (This was the era of the possessive pronoun; no one said "people" any longer. The people had been appropriated; everyone was a possessor of people: our people.) "Our pee–ople," Heiland continued, "our people don't need such things."

"Certainly—but—please understand what I'm trying to say. It is a study, no more than that, a finger exercise, if you will, a little sketch dashed down . . ."

"The sketch of a street," Heiland responded—oh, what presence of mind he had—"is, if you write it down or draw it for yourself, entirely unobjectionable. But you are printing it, or rather you want to have it printed."

"Does that mean that permission is refused?"

"After all, we must look into your intentions and if necessary investigate . . ."

Blumentritt felt the uselessness of this dialogue.

"I've already explained to you: I wanted to give someone pleasure, be able to make a present."

"We must ask ourselves: to whom does such a thing give pleasure? Does a thing like this improve labor morale, the joy in life of our working people? Well then, you describe a street such as scarcely exists any longer among us—or should no longer exist. You speak of a dog, of the bad condition of the pavement, of a puddle of manure water—now what do you mean by all that? Perhaps such a street still exists somewhere outside of Schochern, but in that case we must say . . ." (Era of the eternal "in that case"; era of drawn conclusions, era of clear, prompt judgments, of snap judgments; one thing follows from another; era of "therefores.")

"Inessential details," Blumentritt protested. He had forgotten about the dog.

"Therefore not typical!" Heiland declared. He spoke tersely, tightly: "Don't you also have a taste for formalistic painters? Oh well, let us leave that aside. But you must have been thinking of something when you wrote down —here, for example, at the end: Smoke in the air, a woman, a puddle, a motorcycle roars by—our industry's new motorcycles are very quiet, I must say, so this must be a very old model—I can't imagine that this sort of thing is useful to anyone." He began moving the paper back and forth over the small cleared area in the middle of the desk. "And then this pregnant woman: 'Sometimes one really cannot say what one thinks.' What is that supposed to mean? Who cannot say what he thinks here?"

"That is supposed to mean: She does not know what she thinks. Not that she is not allowed to think. . . . But I really don't care so much about that sentence. I don't care so much about any of it that I . . ."

"And then here! This business by the pond, with the frogs and the young man . . ."

"He is remembering, that's all," Blumentritt said.

"But—throwing stones at frogs?"

"He's annoyed." Blumentritt felt desperate.

"Still and all—we are nature lovers!"

"I can't explain it to you—really not," Blumentritt said conclusively. "With the best will in the world I can't explain it to you—there would be no point and I really don't care so much about it. Let's cut it short: will you or will you not approve it? That is the question."

"Well then—no, I would have to pass it on, send it on up for a decision; this is the first case of this kind."

"Then I'll withdraw it. May I have it back?"

Heiland looked to the right and looked to the left. "I'll send the manuscript back to you; I don't have the original here." He stowed the copies back in his desk.

"Let us talk about something else," Heiland continued in a more conciliatory tone. "Let us talk about the fact that you are an expert in your subject matter, as a teacher, I mean. You keep up with things, and you certainly seem to enjoy it. German, geography, and a little music, too, are your subjects, if I am not mistaken."

"That is true, but I came to see you in order . . ."

"One moment, I don't want to forget this. I have something on my mind. And let us drop this unpleasant subject for the moment—because you will admit that anything like this printing matter is unpleasant for us too. But you do have a command of language, don't you? And how! We can certainly learn something from you there—I've seen some of your letters too—so I know! I know you are skillful, and that kind of talent cannot be overestimated. It can always be put to good use. You're pretty well up on music too, aren't you?"

"A little, I should say."

"Then the name Balthasar Kempff certainly means something to you?"

"I would say so."

"He worked for a long time here, as you know, and now at last we're putting in a memorial to him, just a small room, but at least it's something."

"That's very good to hear. He deserved it," Blumentritt said. He gave up trying to preserve his anger any longer. Perhaps it was better just to let everything pass over him, to put Heiland in a good humor, to agree with him, and an innocuous conversation about Kempff seemed admirably suited to this purpose. "A composer who has received far too little attention!"

"You know his biography? Does he really merit attention?"

"I should say so!" Blumentritt replied. "I know his life quite well; he has considerable importance for the town, or rather vice versa: the town for him."

"So I wasn't mistaken when I thought you one of our most capable teachers."

Blumentritt wanted to fend off the effect this compliment had upon him. But that dreadful shiver—the treacherous happiness of receiving praise—nevertheless ran down his spine; he could not quell it. The face on the wall looked complacently down upon him.

"There is a great deal of fallow ground there," Heiland continued. "A wide field lies open before you." Heiland was choosing his words very carefully, like a doctor exhorting a patient not to fall prey to the lure of cigarettes. And he also spoke like a teacher who from constantly dealing with children ends by no longer regarding adults as altogether mature. In addition, however, he also spoke like a patriarch. It was such rapture to look up to a patriarch and for once, after all the rebukes, to be praised. How could that help but send your spirits soaring! How your spine tingled! How your eyes brimmed with tears of joy when the master caressed and did not punish, lauded and did not scold. What joy to be appreciated.

"You know, these are areas in which you could make yourself useful," Heiland continued, "and I'm sure you will not refuse—when I call upon you to deliver the speech for the dedication of the memorial!"

"But," Blumentritt stammered, disarmed by this new turn of events, "all I really know about is Kempff's musical achievements, not much about the historical aspects . . ." No, impossible! What was being asked of him? A speech? Publicity? What misadventures he might be plunged into; how that would wrench him out of his carefully guarded obscurity. He raised his hands in demur. "But really, you can't really ask me . . ."

"If there's something you don't know, if you need anything, there are books and advisers. Books and advisers! You would accept advice, wouldn't you?"

"Why, of course." No, it wouldn't do, it would lead too far. And then he began to doubt; he considered that he could not refuse the request. Perhaps here was a chance to rectify the damage done by his objectionable literary effort on village streets and frogs. Could it be that the manuscript had already been passed on to higher authorities? Was that the reason it was not at hand? "The task seems almost too much for me," Blumentritt said, humbling himself.

"I can't think of anyone else more suited for it. You need only read up a bit on it, that's all. You don't mean to try to talk yourself out of it . . ."

"Not at all, but I would have to have time to inform myself on several questions of local history . . ." Blumentritt still temporized, seeking a way out; but he had already indicated that he was not unreceptive to the assignment, in principle. Was there any way to escape it now?

A composer! Could any danger lurk in that? Once more he was gripped by that numbing tension he had felt at the beginning of the interview, when he found he could not bring out his grievance. Well then, get to it! Onward, forwards, he must do it, no more faltering, although he was no longer hot but cool under the collar, for the door had opened behind him; Heiland exchanged a glance with someone, perhaps the secretary in the violet dress. Blumentritt did not turn around; he had to focus on his task. "Very well, then," he said, when Heiland again turned his attention toward him, "I'll be glad to deliver the talk, much too great an honor, you know, I was only surprised. . . . And after all I can turn for help to specialists, perhaps Archivist Meiran."

"Oh Lord, Meiran," the mayor replied, and as he lifted his glasses for a second his face looked just a trace more blasted, as though the struggle with a granite mentality, a struggle whose marks he still bore, were about to resume. "That old crank with his writings on the use of the swastika as a decorative emblem, or whatever it was."

"That's not quite his subject."

"Something of the kind. He is one with our enemies, you ought to know. Better not get mixed up with him; he'll tell you nothing but rot; his ideas are worthless."

"Then why was he made archivist after the war?" Blumentritt queried.

"Because we needed him. That's true of a good many people. We cannot do without them until younger ones come along; then they can be 'dumped.' " In which category did he, Blumentritt, fit? "We need younger people; we must put the past behind us."

My cue! Blumentritt thought. "Nevertheless," he said "wasn't he treated unjustly?"

Heiland looked at him as if what Blumentritt had said came under laws of thought altogether alien to the history of mankind—a logic perhaps proper to Mars, or to the Andromeda nebula, or perhaps the logic of dream, in which after and before, cause and effect, are reversed. "What was unjust about it? Forget about the old fellow; he always acted in diametrical opposition to the demands of the times. There is no contradiction in those demands; the contradictions were all in him. He simply exhibited a want of insight and obstinately hung on to outmoded notions. We must put the past behind us."

"My cue!" Blumentritt thought. At last he saw a way to break into this conversation with his problem, which would no longer brook postponement. "You said: put the past behind us. That is just what brought me here. And that has also been the underlying purpose of my—suggestions. But what is happening with that street light is the diametrical opposite. Here you are preserving the past. You know what I mean. You are setting up the gallows again. Or have you forgotten what happened at the end of the war?" He noticed a strange transformation in Heiland's face, a chilling, a paling. The mayor's complexion became almost as waxen as Archivist Meiran's. "Away with the past, certainly! But can we forget it? A man hanged and forgotten!"

Heiland let him finish. Then he said: "Why are you worrying about things that are none of your affair?" No one, he went on, no one beside Blumentritt continued to bother about what had happened, and besides, a lamp post was a lamp post, an object an object.

Here Blumentritt caught him in an error. "Don't we say that a gun is not just a gun? We are always making distinctions . . ."

Silence, a pause, only the rumbling of the steam heat and Heiland's heavy breathing. "You are indulging in dangerous trains of thought there!" Heiland said at last. "I'd like to give you a piece of advice: drop this thing! You can easily get yourself all snarled up on it. You create problems for yourself, question truths . . ."

"What am I questioning? I only say that objects have two aspects, and that the law of killing may perpetuate itself. . . . The memory remains that guns fire and that someone can be strung up on a gallows."

The law of killing! Suspicion germinated in the corners of Heiland's eyes. He scrutinized Blumentritt closely; there was a twitching in his cheeks, but his voice remained low—vibrating as though he were sitting in a softly upholstered car. And he spoke with complete faith in the effectiveness of his words: "You'd better break yourself of that kind of thinking! There is no abstract law of killing; one must always ask: who—whom! Either you

(107

haven't realized that or I must assume that something is concealed behind your words, that you are criticizing for the sake of criticizing. And that is something that can only please the enemy. Understand? Only the enemy! Whom does it serve? You are turning to look backwards; you are far too much concerned with the past; you are only evading; but we must demand that everyone take a position! Therefore I am giving you the opportunity to deliver this speech, in which you can say what things were like then and what they are like today. You must see it all from the standpoint of today; then you will not need so many historical studies; then you will no longer harp on what was but see that all men are happy, we don't want any defeatists, you talk about the law of killing! What's the idea of that, defeatism won't do, or are you allowing yourself to be talked into defeatism—and by whom? You must cut that out, that is what we are asking of you, we are giving you a chance to take part, to go along with us, to take your stand—take your stand!"

Blumentritt heard that the speech was finished. Dismissal now, enough of words, back to the anteroom, out again to the violet woman, past Frau Zergaden, the suction of her glance at his back, out once more: here at last in the open air came the recognition that he had let himself in for something the consequences of which he could not foresee. What had he done to please the enemy? A triviality, a foolish triviality, Blumentritt; you may well be surprised. He was very depressed that he had undertaken to deliver the speech; he regretted that he had ever entrusted any sketches to the printer; and he felt entangled, discomfited, only half recalled what he had actually said; was surrounded by gray emptiness—and weariness, intense weariness.

Go away and forget, everything, the smoke, the city, the fogginess of the day—get through this day, go away, simply take a trip somewhere; traveling gives you the illusion that you cannot be located—or else sink back into yourself like a sick person whom noise no longer reaches, act no longer, talk no longer, simply be, wait, let the fog rise (and the night and the day and again the night, a year, two years)—watch when the colors lighten, hope to shake off the smells and dust of the town, pay them no mind, breathe faster and make noise, start to drink again, distract yourself, perhaps that helps, drinking, keep on drinking, absorb something that numbs this terrible craving for something indefinable—but it doesn't help, drinking is foolish, nothing works, nothing numbs me but Luminal, no matter how much I drink, I remain sober, nothing distracts me, every attempt fails. And how gladly I would run away from events. Now Kumtsiel has been arrested; there's always something new and nothing good, as people say, and what's it like when a man like that suddenly disappears? The first day he's missed, but by the second he's missed no longer; a new principal has been installed. But it doesn't make sense; I thought Kumtsiel a reliable man, a disciplined adherent of the system, not bothered by doubts. Why in the world was he arrested? Did it have anything to do with the pupils who supposedly set fire to a banner? I don't know, nobody knows, but nobody defends him. Anyone who disappears is guilty, whereas anyone who is still here or returns is cleared: that was what happened to Grünmeissel. Grünmeissel is back. Grünmeissel has become the shooting instructor, hard to believe, but what's the use of mulling over it, I'm no longer capable of amazement. Grünmeissel was added to the faculty without anyone's raising the slightest objection. Or had there been some objection I wasn't aware of? Had Kumtsiel objected? Who knows what's going on; who would venture to talk about it? I remember the day Grünmeissel returned from the internment camp and I stood opposite him, unexpectedly I stood opposite him and he recognized his former pupil. "Dead," he whispered to me; I thought he had gone out of his mind. What did he mean? "Dead! Don't you notice that everything is dead?" His garlic breath grazed me; I did not have the courage to let him stand there on the street and to go right past him without a greeting; perhaps he was mad, perhaps imprisonment had broken him psychically, for he only said again and again: "Dead! Everything is dead!" Then he walked on. After that I sometimes greeted him on the street—you never know quite how to behave toward sick people, even when you don't like them; but he seemed to recover quickly. He never again spoke to me or pelted me with such statements. Gradually I lost sight of him; during the next few years he must have changed, and now he is sitting opposite me in the faculty room and is again teaching the boys shooting. Perhaps it doesn't matter that it's Grünmeissel; someone else would be found to teach them how to use the gunsight, and why do I let myself get all worked up. I ought to stop that, ought to greet Grünmeissel cordially, as my colleagues do. There was no objection, no one opposed the new reality—what would be the point? It would change nothing and would have pleased nobody if one of us had raised a fuss about Grünmeissel's appointment. It would only have disturbed the smooth progress of the meeting. Wasn't Grünmeissel relieving us of the bothersome duty of teaching the boys how to shoot?

The meeting proceeded in complete concord. The new principal sat at the head of the table and looked around, shrewdly, craftily. Unanimity creates contentment, no doubt about it. In the end Grünmeissel had his class, the schedules had been changed, satisfaction on everyone's face. I took a pack of cigarettes from my pocket and offered it to Grünmeissel across the table, but he refused; he was still a non-smoker, as he used to be, he said; didn't I remember. Of course, I said, I remembered very well. And that he also kept away from alcohol on principle, he said. Certainly, I said. Highly praiseworthy, the new principal said. That saved a lot of money, a month's salary in a year, some of the others joked; that was the way to get ahead. Everyone has his vice, Grünmeissel said; his vice was eating chocolate. But then, why not, the principal said. Indeed, why not. I stuck a cigarette between my lips. We all went out together to the schoolyard; the school was to take part in a parade. Since I had no matches with me, I put the cigarette back in the pack.

Two pupils from my class stepped forward from the line of march. "This is your banner," they said.

At first I thought it was a joke. "My banner?" I asked.

Yes, it was for me and one of the other teachers. They held out to me the two wooden staffs with the cloth stretched between them. But what was I to do with it? Carry a banner? Perhaps while Grünmeissel held the other end! "Leave me out of it, I really can't today," I said. They were taken aback. "Go on." Then they thrust the banner upon someone else—I don't know whom. I took my place at the end of the line (I cannot keep up much of a pace because of my leg); but this time I completely lost my group; the boys ran away from me, and other contingents came between us when we arrived in the center of town. Where was I? What had I been thinking of? At the Fish Market I could not find my unit of the parade, I was caught in the general confusion and blocked from making any further progress. What this demonstration was about, what the pretext for it was, I did not discover, for each demonstration is like the other; the speeches are all alike and are scarcely listened to. People stand around in groups and chat, the loudspeaker roars and fails and whistles, and when there is a moment of silence, it is filled by applause. I listened a while, clapped, and slipped away to one side—as always.

Later I found two of my pupils waiting at my door. They disturb me with their digressive restlessness, but I rather like that; I don't try to discourage their visits, even encourage them, and they come often. This time they were two of the youngest: Schunke and tubby little Timm. Schunke is the district attorney's son, and Timm's father is a cutter in a textile house. What do the two of them, this ill-assorted pair, want?

"Friendship, Herr Blumentritt," Schunke greets me, and Timm adds his voice: "Friendship." I repeat the greeting; that is the custom, although it's hard to see the point of the word nowadays. "Herr Blumentritt," they ask me, "we're supposed to send packages to the West. We've got the addresses." They tell me where they obtained the addresses—from some district office, but what they want me to tell them is: "What do we put in the packages?" Haven't they been told, I ask. No, they don't know, and so I explain that it depends on whom the packages are meant for. "If they are children, send toys," I say, "because it will soon be Easter."

Schunke has other ideas. "Fats," he says.

But Timm does not agree. "They've got everything in the West!"

How can he say that to Schunke? Sure enough, Schunke lashes out at him: "You're a reactionary; we must promote the struggle for peace." And I have to witness the little squabble for a moment because I am not nimble enough to intervene.

"If they get enough to eat, they won't fight," Timm avers. "That's something you don't know." He claims to have heard that from his father. "Recently my Dad came home and said: 'They're waiting here for the depression that's supposed to start over there. Without a depression we get nowhere. Without a depression nothing will happen. Those who have their bellies full won't go out on the streets for us.' " The political instructor had told him that, confidentially. " 'First they've got to have it real tough. Otherwise we can wait forever.' So there! If they're supposed to have things real tough," Timm pursued his argument, "why should we send them fats?"

What put this into his mind? Schunke will certainly take alarm. I reprove Timm: "It surely was not meant that way; you've not understood it correctly."

And Schunke explains: "He doesn't understand anything, Herr Blumentritt. He sticks up for the Fascists and the militarists."

But I hardly allow him to finish his sentence, for that is also going too far. I distract them by repeating that toys are probably best, or else books. "Brecht, Thomas Wolfe," Timm offers by way of commentary. Oh yes, he understands about books. I've noticed that; these fellows are informed about all the newest publications, and yet he's a workingman's boy—it's amazing. Incidentally, at the moment I don't recall whether he really said Thomas Wolfe. I'm certain about Brecht; the other writer might have been Borchert. At any rate, Schunke promptly throws in: "Brecht and Borchert"—or Wolfe, I'm no longer sure—"are license editions; we're not allowed to send them." He thinks for a while. "I know," he exclaims. "We'll send cardboard models of tanks and planes; they can play with them and they're easy to mail."

I am only taken aback, but Timm laughs. What is there to laugh at? "You see who's the militarist now?" He turns to Schunke again. "I thought you were so against them for displaying cannon and military toys in the shop windows in West Germany. You wrote that in a composition last week."

I have already raised a pacifying hand and am expecting Schunke to flare up again, but he only says: "That's right," and considers. "Then what can we send?" He has posed himself an intellectual problem that he cannot cope with, and I admit that I too have no ready answer. Finally Schunke comes forth with a new suggestion: "Now I have it. All we have is T-34's and Migs, and they're to defend peace."

But Timm replies scornfully: "Suppose they don't realize that over there?"

(115

Schunke insists: "We've got to explain to them how to use them. After all, there's only one way to play with T-34's."

Timm does not give up. "But suppose we send them to the wrong people? How do we know?"

Schunke's resignation is genuine. "It's just too complicated. We never know what to do; everything is wrong."

I grant that there are uncertainties which exceed the capacity of a boy's mind. I am unspeakably weary and empty after this episode; I send them away, go to my desk, reach for a book, put it aside again. I am thirsty and hungry, would like to distract my mind, don't even know what I am thirsty and hungry for—it is only the old restiveness again, the old insatiability, and at times I think that I am not the only one who feels this way; I have the impression that people eat and drink only because they do not see why they should not eat and drink. To quench that thirst finally! But I am insatiable. Why do I drink without ever quenching my thirst? Why do I eat without ever feeling filled? There are nights when I throw all moderation to the winds, and by day I control myself only by intense effort. Yet I do not drink to get drunk, quite aside from the fact that I can scarcely ever succeed. Nor do I prefer the really strong beverages which stir desires rather than appease them, and which people drink quite aside from any thirst. No, this craving has nothing to do with my thirst. My thirst is different in kind; it extends beyond this and the next glass of any sparkling drink, or any wine, to the next after next; it clings to drinking and is renewed by it; it is a thirst that grows with drinking, a craving for food that increases with the quantity eaten. My thirst is roused to the point of agony by the sight of a flowing fountain; I cannot sit in a movie house and look on without groaning when actors drink on the screen. I avoid the sight of a river rushing bright and brisk in the springtime under a bridge, or a sluggish pond with a puffy, purling surface. And I know that what affects me is the quantity, apart from anything specific, apart from any essence or taste; it is always the quantity. But to gulp down a quantity, in between to take a bite of something, anything, and then to drink again when the satisfaction in work wears off, when I can scarcely force myself to go on sitting at the desk, and when my palate has become dry from repeated cigarettes. This boundless thirst, which only feeds itself, inevitably leads to disgust. I know. I have states in which it becomes impossible for me to eat or drink anything at all; but this disgust does not last long. Pretty soon the bottomless craving returns. No one has so much rationality at his command that he can keep the feeling of disgust constantly in mind, so that he adjusts to a permanent abstinence. No use attempting that. Every effort fails. And who is to think about the causes? How would you go about analyzing them? Where are they to be found? I have no notion; I cannot even recall any longer when it all began.

Inez blames it on narrowness. Or on fear? Inez has an explanation for everything, even for the fact that she has an explanation for everything. Women see things differently, you know, she says. Yet she eats constantly, and of late she has begun to gain weight too. Justifications, analyses—none of them accounts for the hunger, none for the thirst. Inez blames it all on the narrowness of our life; she talks about surrogate religions, and includes eating among them.

Go away and forget? If only one could. Just once, at least, to flee the smoke and the mistiness of the day, to go away, take a trip (you won't survive this day), simply to go somewhere (where?), to sink back like a sick man whom noise no longer reaches, to contract oneself into a single point, no longer go roaming about, simply to stay still, to wait, to let the mists rise (and the night and the day and again the night), to wait and see, shake off the smells and the dust and the vapors (it is not fog, only vapors, only dust), shake it all off and wait without a thought, or else breathe faster and make noise, join the crowd, start drinking again, take part, be distracted, perhaps that will help, drink, go on drinking forever, downing something that will anesthetize this fearful thirst for something indefinable, for something dependable; or better still: stop breathing altogether, rest.

Blumentritt would not have been surprised to awaken one morning and find himself a midget, as happens at times in certain stories; or else, to go into his bedroom

at night a perfectly normal, upright man, master of his own
decisions, to go to bed and—but his forebodings went no
further. He took Luminal—the habitual reaching out to
the night table for the glass of water, for the medicine,
while still half asleep; and as he slowly pulled himself
together, his thoughts centered on how he was to work
up his speech; he could not afford to let his mind dwell on
other things. Time was moving so quickly and people were
already beginning to talk. Frau Luja brought him his
coffee: "So you are going to give a speech?" Yes, he was
going to, only he did not yet know how. And Inez asked
him when she next saw him: "Did you have to? It's in the
newspaper." Of course, he might have expected that, and
after all, what did it signify? Only the customers in
Karwenka's Art Shop probably could not forebear from
making such remarks as: Well, well, that teacher, always
seemed a likable fellow, what's his name again, I hear he's
joined the speechmakers—you heard anything about it?
Such talk was carefully planted; there was no one who had
not heard that Blumentritt frequented the place; in Schochern nothing could be kept secret. And when Blumentritt
passed by old Metzeki, who always smelled of tinder, pipes,
and tar, and the old man stood still and turned around—
nodding, to be sure, with approval or not, but nodding,
fierce satisfaction in his eyes—then Blumentritt wondered:
did he know something too? Blumentritt became insecure,
he lived in fear of another anonymous letter; but none
came. Possibly, too, most people understood him and said

to themselves: Good thing that he's making the speech and not someone else. Or else they were just waiting to see what the outcome would be. And the more Blumentritt delved into the subject, the more reconciled he became to his task, the more he felt himself a citizen of the town that had brought him forth (brought forth Balthasar Kempff, brought forth Blumentritt). And the more he read about Kempff, the more he liked Schochern.

He borrowed books from Meiran. The archivist lived on Wilmschlucht, the street that ran parallel to the river. There, against one wing of a house surrounding a paved courtyard, a wooden staircase ran up to the two rooms inhabited by Meiran and his dog with the herbal name. The rooms were crammed with mementos of a collector's life: plates, engravings, sketch maps, pewter mugs, stones from various historic sites, painted peasant furniture. Among the latter was an old secretary desk with folio volumes open on it (there was no saying whether Meiran had just been reading them), and in the other room, which held an old army cot, were bookshelves to the ceiling. The archivist, in his green corduroy jacket, was more than helpful. He chased the dachshund Majoran under the bed, and went through his library picking out volumes containing material on the court and customs of the time, on festivals, organs, librettists, and musicians. He made notes, inserted slips of paper into books, sorted, carried stuff away, cleared out a whole drawer solely to find a faded pamphlet containing Kempff's letters to the court, and filled his two small rooms with bustling activity, as though he were the one who had been asked to speak, as though he had been restored to his post of honor. At times, however, he seemed to become suspicious of the whole affair, and then he would raise his eyes from a pile of books and stare at Blumentritt with astonishment and incredulity. When Blumentritt took his leave, Meiran once again set the complicated machinery of his facial muscles in motion: brow furrowing, eyes opening and closing, eyebrows raising, eyelids flickering, finally eyes rolling—a form of stammering in pantomine: "Well, 'Woman Arising' is gone. Didn't I tell you?" he declared triumphantly. "This means Inez is playing along with Heiland; she's let him pilfer the Zergaden woman, and 'Woman Arising' as well." Blumentritt, already at the door, protested the idea; he said only a few words and left. Behind him the corduroy jacket scuffed and the dachshund barked.

Blumentritt was having his troubles with people. He could not make out the new principal. The man always spoke to him—why him—about the annoyance the parents' advisory committee was causing him; there was that district attorney Schunke on the committee who was always going on about criticism and self-criticism, ha-ha-ha, nothing but annoyances, the principal maintained; and after this brief peal of laughter he would swiftly grow sad. He was considerably younger than Blumentritt, and why did he always go to him with the stories of the annoyances and Schunke and self-criticism, ha-ha?

Blumentritt also had his troubles with flowers. It happened this way. One day he had to tell the printer that he was canceling his order. The printer, Pfannstiel, had leathery skin and a wrinkled throat. He moved his aging head back and forth like a cock. He had one problematical trait—he was unable to keep abreast of the current situation. And that the authorities should have refused a license for Blumentritt's little piece, why that was, that could not, how could . . . "No, what ith the idea!" he lisped—he was losing the job, too, although that did not matter so much. "I don't underthtand that. What can they have againtht it? While they're about it, they may ath well get rid of flowerth!" Why flowers, Blumentritt asked; what did he mean by that. "Well, flowerth are thomething eth-thetic too," the printer said. "I never get anything eth–thetic to print any more. Didn't uthe to be that way. But if eth–thetic thtuff ain't allowed any more, they might ath well ban flowerth and be done with it."

Blumentritt tried to explain that there was a considerable difference between nature and language, that he had described something, whereas flowers only gave out scent. "Don't you thmell this here?" Pfannstiel patted his palm on a copy he had kept for himself, which lay on the narrow wooden shelf in his office. "Didn't you dethcribe thomething so that a perthon can thmell it?" And besides it was meant for giving away, just like flowers. . . . It was simply impossible to demonstrate the difference; the printer remained uncomprehending. Again and again

Pfannstiel voiced his disbelief in the decision of the authorities, urged Blumentritt to try again, perhaps they'd only
made a mistake, surely that couldn't be their last word on
something eth–thetic, and if he weren't allowed to print
such a thing flowerth might as well be . . .

So that was a source of annoyance, and then there was
the problem of the speech. It cost him a good many restless nights, and he could forsee that his uncertainty would
last until it was all over. But gradually the character of
Balthasar Kempff became real to him. That slow growth
toward monumentality, the attainment of a Biblical age,
and what a death, surrounded by singing friends and
children. But it wouldn't do to dwell too much on that.
Blumentritt read and read, and one night, lying sleepless
in bed, he saw why Kempff had allowed himself to become so deeply involved with Schochern. During the
Thirty Years' War Kempff had left the town several
times. Later he longed to put his life's affairs in order at
last, to build a citadel around his work, so that it would be
preserved. There was no one far and wide who had
understood the meaning of his work and realized what it
needed: musicians, a chorus, the human voice, community,
something which the work itself epitomized. And so he
had fought for citizenship and had also fought for his house
(in which the memorial was now to be established), not

so much as property, but as a place of homecoming for a wanderer, one cast adrift by the war. He had fought for an external standard for his life which would be in keeping with his internal standard. And here, perhaps, lay the pivot for Blumentritt's speech, here at this midpoint in Kempff's life. Blumentritt got out of bed in the middle of the night, went to his desk, and wrote.

During the following days he did nothing but revise. Incessantly, he made revisions, altered sentence after sentence, not so much out of dissatisfaction as out of caution —for so many little things kept creeping in. Kempff had usually based his works on Biblical texts, and these in themselves were dubious. A phrase which Blumentritt thought trenchant one day, he struck out the next, and sentences that yesterday had seemed obscure and ambiguous appeared today as too blatant, too direct. Toward evening, after hours of considering and reconsidering, he would step out into the tangle of narrow streets, where forgetfulness came more easily, where he could rest his mind from the travail of thought. Or else he went to Inez; she knew what best relaxed him, what made him forget. Talk was scarcely necessary; they came together quickly each time, but even as they lay silent and happily tired side by side, he began to brood again, thinking about the new principal, about Kumt, whose arrest and disappearance still preoccupied him (no one commented on the case); and he considered how strange it was when you yourself suddenly vanished and no one was permitted to comment about you, since no one knew anything specific; and if the trial came, you were sure to be guilty. Once more he reviewed the question of whether there was sufficient evidence against himself for an indictment. Ridiculous. A little descriptive piece, petitions to the authorities, pictures in his room; he had been warned, had received a letter and not reported it, had made a few difficulties about accepting the assignment for the speech. When Inez saw that he was being silent too long and thinking too hard (she watched his face), she got up and dressed, and later she accompanied him, a little sadly, out to the garden gate, and he went home, across the whole town from Crooked Hill, each time taking a different route. Sometimes he became lost in parts of the town which he normally never entered.

Once he heard a voice calling his name: Blu–men–tritt! He thought it must be an illusion, until the call was repeated: Blu–men–tritt! Where had it come from? It seemed to come from the mountain that loomed up close to the town, at this point; he was not far from the old Knacker's Yard, near which the house of Balthasar Kempff was situated. Blumentritt halted in front of a gate; the voice seemed to be calling from behind it: Blu–men–tritt! He stepped across the wooden threshold, but the courtyard behind the gate was empty. The place was a coalyard; here, when Blumentritt was a boy, the black princess had lived. That was what they called the coal dealer's daughter, who rode through town on her father's cart, sitting beside the driver and urging the horses on with her whip, and when boys approached too close to suit her, she reached behind her into the mound of coal and tossed sharp-edged coal at them. She looked almost like a boy, with a slender, still undeveloped body; but she had a face like a princess, skin white as smoke, black eyes, black hair, and everywhere in the hollows and pores of that white skin smudges of coal dust. Blumentritt went on; he walked faster, raised his eyes, searching, and as he turned into another street he lost his sense of direction for a moment. The call came from this street—so he thought—but where did the street go? As he advanced, the unexpected happened: he saw a girl running away, scurrying around a corner. The black princess, he thought; but that was impossible; he was mixing up the planes of time; Blumentritt, pull yourself together, the black princess, the coalman's daughter, is as old as you are today, perhaps older, fairly old anyhow, and probably a matron and hideous, fat and heavy, if she's still living at all; that girl can't be she. Who was it? Perhaps the call was not meant for him at all; but for someone else with a similar name; the girl was fleeing from a stranger, not from him; or else she was teasing him. He strode forward, walked uphill; the street led into the district around the castle. He stumbled a bit, and then again, quite plainly, he heard his name: Blu-men-tritt! But how was it possible, could he be so mistaken— was that fleeing figure Frau Zergaden, her boy's body, her hermaphroditic withered self? He hurried after her, but in vain; she was faster than he; he was much too clumsy, a limping fool, an unfortunate acrobat who'd lost his balance. And the person he was pursuing with childish scampers was surely not Frau Zergaden. . . . The call came once more from the maze of the streets, so it seemed to him, and then he'd gone wrong, run into a blind alley; he walked back, stumbling down steps, past the gray rear walls of houses, turned once to the left, once to the right.

Blu–men–tritt! Herr Blumentritt! the voice called this time. "Good God, man, don't you hear? It's me, behind you!" Blumentritt turned around; a moment ago there had been nothing, no one, he'd come out of a deserted alley. And there, behind him, stood Fenk. "I only wanted to ask you—if you don't mind—if you still blame me for that, I mean, you know what I'm referring to, about the boy— do stand still for a moment!—that I complained about you —let me finish, for God's sake!—that I complained about you and maybe made trouble for you and . . ."

"All right, all right, Herr Fenk. There are more important things to think about. Best if you never refer to it again."

But Fenk was to refer to it again several times.

A speech more or less, it added nothing, took nothing away. Only he wished the day were over and done with; he wished that it did not exist, or that he himself did not exist. Suppose he suddenly didn't, or he became ill and the celebration was called off. But that did not happen. He read his speech again and again, turned it this way and that, tried to hear how it would sound in the ears of others, what its effect would be, and how it would be taken by this person and that—but came to no conclusion.

Publicity! If only he could have descended again into the anonymous crowd; that would have been better, not to be a teacher, to be no one, an unwritten page. He would have given anything to be nameless, unknown to the authorities, not a teacher with certain things to his credit, an anti-Fascist mentioned a good many times on public occasions. No, to be a grain of dust, unknown to all, with no one paying attention to him. Or else, to be able to descend once more into the daydream of childhood, into the lowly existence of any chance creature under God's heaven, not marked by shame and lies (we are always lying) and controversial actions.

But that was no longer possible. On the appointed day he took his sheaf of papers—after reading the speech for the tenth time he no longer had the slightest idea of its effect—and went to the Knacker's Yard, where the erstwhile house of Balthasar Kempff awaited its new fate. The name of the neighborhood was no longer Knacker's Yard, of course (but then Crooked Hill was no longer called that either; what's in a name). A plaque had meanwhile been installed at the house, right beside the entrance to the laundry room, ground floor, left. There Balthasar

Kempff had lived. The plaque was still draped. But the solemn ceremony of unveiling the memorial plaque could not, of course, take place on the street. Consequently they went three houses down the street and into the Red Horse. There was a public hall at the rear of the Red Horse. Student drinking bouts and club dances were part of the reactionary prehistory of the Red Horse. At present the hall was available only for meetings: the proprietor did not want to bring new taxes down upon himself by offering amusements and dances. He would rather do with smaller profits. Clubs no longer existed; a hall like this could only be rented for official ceremonies for a fixed fee. The lectern and the laurels were left over from the last meeting; the wall decorations were always the same.

Toward five o'clock in the afternoon the hall filled. The representatives of the authorities sat in the front rows, on the left, because the town clergy and the organists had seated themselves on the right. They too regarded Balthasar Kempff as one of their own (hopeless to try untangling *that* complication). Blumentritt went up to the chair which had been reserved for him. Heiland rose to greet him. Blumentritt shook hands with the mayor; he merely nodded to the clergy. He sat exactly between the parties, between Heiland and the official Protestant minister. He held his rolled-up speech clutched in his restless hand. He guarded it like a secret which had not yet revealed itself even to him. Now he had to stand up once more; Heiland introduced him to Spillner, the museum head, who stammered out a phrase: He had already heard of him! What had he heard? Blumentritt grew even more uncomfortable, as he thought of his speech, for here was this bulbous-headed fellow and there were the ministers and Heiland with the violet woman from his anteroom, and far to the back, in the last row, sat Meiran in his corduroy jacket, chin pressed against his throat, brow furrowed. Well then. Blumentritt glanced over the rows once more, and recognized Kummerbart's heirs, brother and sister, right behind the clergy.

The speeches began. Blumentritt had imagined that there would be only a few brief words of introduction and then he would have to speak. But far from it. Municipal representatives stood up to cite various accomplishments; envoys and delegates from factories and organizations put forth their own proprietary rights to Balthasar Kempff; half an hour passed and Heiland had not yet delivered his remarks, after which the festival address was scheduled. Why wasn't Onion-head saying something? He would have been the logical speaker, but he gave no sign of getting to his feet. What kind of man was he anyhow?

There was no end in sight. At last Heiland spoke, but he too made no headway. It was growing dark outside, and still Heiland, wandering far from the subject at hand, went on listing the various glories of the town (we have a monument for the friend of the deaf-mutes the great progressive pedagogue who arose out of modest circumstances a son of the people and whose needs he understood and the needs and distress of the deaf-mutes that is to say they really should be called the hard of hearing, deaf-mutes is wrong it is not that they are mute their problem is that they do not hear, well then we have a monument)—Heiland went on praising the cultural heritage of the town.

There was coughing in the hall; people shuffled their feet. Heiland was not exactly popular, that was clear, and parenthetically Blumentritt recalled a phrase: He'll hang first, people said. Probably that was the reason Blumentritt had made a fool of himself when he urged his neighbors on the Fish Market to join in an action against the lamp post; they'd smiled ever so faintly when he used the word *gallows*. A gallows can always be put to use, they'd said; there have to be gallows, some people hang first. Possibly they did not mean that seriously, but it gave you an insight; Blumentritt's arguments broke against their irony; and perhaps some of them were sitting here in the hall, coughing and scuffling their feet. What would they think of his speech? Finally Heiland praised the town's wisdom in purchasing a sculpture by Kummerbart; the municipality had made it possible for this impressive art work to be set up in the cemetery. It was a symbol of the general upsurge: *Woman Arising!* So did the people arise, pressing forward toward happy times, until the sun shone for everyone and no one need any longer weep for a lost son. Powerful, vigorous art. Art of the people. Strengthening the people in their struggle, their *Kampf*, and Kempff, and in saying this he had come to the object of this celebration, to the end of his remarks, and hence to the festival address. Herr Blumentritt!

Was he to speak now, after all that! He felt in the wrong place, compromised in advance; all his efforts had been in vain. It wouldn't do; who would listen now, who would pay attention to subtleties; after such a speech, it was well-nigh impossible to proceed. He did so nevertheless; perhaps he would be able to shorten his speech, to skip certain passages. And so he stood up, hunched his shoulders, leaned his cane against the chair, limped slowly to the lectern, and suddenly became conscious of the silence, the slowed breathing of the audience. He leafed through his pages, smoothed them out, was tempted to improvise an introduction, to say he would cut the matter short and tell only a little of the composer's life—but then he abandoned the idea; he was not the man for extemporaneous speeches. He leafed through the pages, laid the manuscript in proper order on the lectern, tried to fix his eyes on one or two faces and read their expression, hoping that one or another would show intimations of good will, so that he need not start without any prospects at all, rejected and condemned before he had been heard. But he could make nothing out of the faces; the minister bowed his head, Kummerbart's heirs stared at the ceiling in sheer vapidity, and Meiran was nowhere to be seen. Blumentritt lifted his brows, began; his throat choked up, he coughed to clear it, his hands shook. Heiland's face glittered, stony cold, in a thin thread of light.

"The atmosphere that arises out of the past," Blumentritt began, and coughed, "which we would wish to evoke
for this inaugural celebration—memorial celebration," he
corrected himself, "the scenes we are commemorating, are
not elevated occasions, moments of destiny, birth and
death, beginnings or radiant consummations." Rather, he
went on, he wished to summon up the everyday life of
a middle-class man of three hundred years ago. A musician
struggles for his livelihood, tries to achieve his independence of the Court of the Electoral Prince, shuts himself off from the world, but without abandoning the
world, for he has cried out against its wretchedness often
enough. But now his own personal wretchedness is so great
that he can no longer do so. He wants to rest, wants to
settle down; he is old enough, has suffered enough at the
court. Such was Blumentritt's exposition. Conditions were
not good in those days, certainly not; those were days of
defeat, days of troubled conscience and seeming hopeless-
ness—good Lord, why was he stressing all this, right at
the beginning of his speech? The implications of this had
escaped him during his rereadings; but Heiland nodded
and Blumentritt went on to describe what had happened to
Balthasar Kempff: how the composer became involved in
conflict with the Electoral Prince, who wanted to take him
away from Schochern and who possessed more power than
the Count of Schochern, who was supporting Kempff.
"A hopeless situation: with this burden upon his shoulders, torn between power and his personal mission"—was
it safe to say that? Was it wise to put it that way, to stress

that personal mission had a claim superior to that of power? Blumentritt expurgated a sentence; he must be on his guard; he no longer knew whom he was offending more, the pastors or Heiland. "We must picture him in his room on the Knacker's Yard, the room with the bay window, from which he was to be expelled," Blumentritt continued. "He bends over the challenging blankness of his music paper, which his eye has already filled with the patterns of new sonorities. But the house does not belong to him; at any time he may fall between the two stools; he is at home nowhere, and his greatest desire is to settle down at last, to build a sheltering wall around his work. Perhaps this very year, this very month, he was completing the final strains of that three-voiced motet with the mighty thunder of the cry: Saul, Saul, why persecutest thou me?"

Now it was out. Blumentritt had raised his voice considerably, and suddenly he felt frightened. Why? After all, it had to be said, only it sounded strange. Yet the motet was one of the greatest works Kempff had left to posterity. The clergymen looked up. Blumentritt forged on. "Or else his thoughts raced ahead of his time to the song of the three men in the fiery furnace, that great work of his old age! But again and again restlessness invaded him. The undecided struggle between the two courts affected him constantly. No man can work under such circumstances; neither time nor place can be found for the bold, free leaps of creativity. What is he to do? Angrily, he pushes the music paper aside, without having made progress. Such sterility is alien to his persevering, self-disciplined character. The grooves in his face, running down from the corners of his mouth and outlining his beard, marking his brow with parallel lines—those furrows familiar to us from pictures—deepen. So we must picture him: unable to concentrate on his work."

The speech seemed to creep along. Why was he trying to draw a portrait of the composer? Why was he sketching in the conflict of the man's life? If only he had limited himself to a few fragments of biography, to a few meaningless phrases! But now he was in the middle of it and there was no turning back; he had built up too much suspense and must tell the audience how the struggle ended. "He poured out his distress in letters. Reluctant though I am, he wrote, to trouble Your Serene Highness with my repeated petitions and memoranda, I am nevertheless impelled by such manifold anxieties and cast down by such piteous wretchedness that I do not know how I should ever hope for betterment of my circumstances, to the which may God testify!" The minister leaned forward in his first-row seat, propped his elbows on his knees, and supported his chin in outspread fingers. Heiland looked at the ceiling.

"Such were his words," Blumentritt said, "and you will understand what I—or rather he—had in mind when you consider that a few weeks after this letter a new deed was made out for the house on the Knacker's Yard! Certified by the town clerk and a council of burgesses. A struggle that had gone on for years was approaching its end; a deed of gift had been bestowed which provided Balthasar Kempff civic rights and security, which offered him a home and a refuge. A refuge!" Blumentritt raised his voice. "And yet fifteen years before he had had to flee from these parts, so inhospitable had they been rendered by the Thirty Years' War. That was, if you will, the first self-exile practiced by an artist in modern times." And Blumentritt described how the composer had gone to Italy to study under Gabrieli and Monteverdi, how he had returned, found no homeland left, and had fled once more; how he had wrestled with his vision of the world, this man endowed with a superlative sense of form, but who when his heart was broken also knew how to protest! When he saw the misery after the war, the condition of the arts, he wrote letters of singular passion. But his perseverance won out! He was able to resist the Electoral Prince; his work triumphed, found generous protection within the walls of his own town. He learned to conceive of it as mission and annunciation, and carried it to its completion in a spirit of profound devoutness. Thus not only his works of art, but the work of art which his life was, matured until he reached the advanced Biblical age . . .

Blumentritt had come to this point when he saw Meiran's head bobbing up above the rows of the audience. Was he on the wrong track? Meiran smiled. Perhaps he was remembering the West German scholar who had

caused all the flurry by mentioning the Count of Schochern; but Blumentritt did not wish to go into that particular portion of Kempff's life. He skipped another few
sentences which dealt in too great detail with Kempff's religious feelings, and launched directly into the grand
summing up—although he feared that he had already lost
his balance, that he had overreached himself in this assignment, exposed himself to attacks from all sides and entangled himself in countless contradictions. If only nothing
dangerous came out now, at the end! This tightrope-
walking was ghastly.

"A blessed tenacity of purpose went into this monu-
mental work, blessed when we consider what barbarous
times the man confronted. Could his strength have sprung
from a conscious moral surmounting of his times? Is the
individual stronger than . . ." Blumentritt, what a tyro
you are on the tightrope! Blumentritt on the trapeze!
Blumentritt waving paper, holding tight to the history of
music over his head, Blumentritt preparing to leap, attention, roll of drums, silence for the great leap forward and
the swing through the air on a history of music. . . .
"Stronger than his times? It remains a wonder, it remains
the sole consolation" (no, that was going too far) "that
a personality like Balthasar Kempff can grow, can reach
to us across murderous epochs, across war and misery,
devastation and violence, like a message of hope. For how
can violence better be overcome than" (careful, you'll
miss the rope, silence) "than in the ordered freedom of

(137

the work of art and in its gentle persuasiveness?" Shudders ran down Blumentritt's spine; the abyss yawned to either side of his rope. The hall was perfectly still—no shuffling of feet could be heard. But how could he ever have written down those words or let them cross his lips! His forehead burned; he hurried on, breathing hard, while Heiland's face remained expressionless and the only movement in the hall was that of the town minister leaning back again.

"Let us summon to mind once more that moment when Kempff sat without hope in his small room with its bay window, steeling himself to lose even this refuge. In the world outside the slaughter of nations goes on, and savage hatred rages in the hearts of men; and here one man sits in his monklike cell, wielding the pen and overcoming the times"—last roll of drums, silence, now there are only two courses: either to lower his voice in order to underplay all that follows, or to place his trust in voice alone, to stun the audience with the impact of his words so that they will have no afterthoughts about the meaning. Blumentritt chooses the second course; it seems to him that he has ruined himself anyhow; he did not adequately consider how you could twist yourself up among allusions. On paper everything seems so innocuous. "Wields the pen, overcoming the times, and in his beautiful, precise handwriting he sets down beneath the still damp page of notes the words of the song of the men in the fiery furnace— for there is added glory to the thought that he was composing this very work at the time! All art begins with praise, and in Kempff too praise only occasionally alternated with lament, the lament that bursts forth when the thunderous storm, the fourteen-voiced full chorus begins with the cry: Saul, Saul, why persecutest thou me? It will be hard for thee to kick against the pricks." It will be hard for thee, Blumentritt, but go on, those aren't your words, after all, they are the words of Kempff; you can talk yourself out of it; it is his work; he composed it as he sat in the house on the Knacker's Yard, so you are entitled to speak of it, only keep going, move on. "The small chamber is filled with the questioning wrath of the basses and tenors; altos and sopranos tower above the thin line of the instruments, and in the distance, in the darkness of his own heart, the voices reverberate, they sound still, ever and again new and living to us, comforting and shattering at one and the same time; and out of the rising wrath Kempff returns in the song of the three men to the simple certainty of things, where it is said that they should praise the Lord: you sun and moon, you stars in the sky, you rain and dew, you day and night, you hoarfrost and snow, you mountains and hills, you birds under heaven, you children of men—and with these words from his lips, these propitiatory words of universal brotherhood" (impossible; this slip of the pen is disastrous) "we step into the sanctuary of his life."

It was done; at the end he had nearly been out of breath, but he had finished. For good or ill, it could no longer be changed now. He folded up his papers; the crackling sound could be heard plainly in the hall, for as yet everyone's hands were still; and while the applause timidly began and swelled, fluttered high like a flock of startled birds, and while Blumentritt's ears roared, he did not even know whether the applause was the cause of it, he stumbled back to his chair, between Heiland and the town minister, and almost fell because in walking he leaned to the right, as he was wont to, but this time he had no cane to support him. What followed scarcely reached his conscious mind. Some music by the municipal quartet and some murmuring at his back, and somewhere in the course of this the minister's hand resting on his.

In this condition of giddy daze, he let himself drift in a group of guests as far as the house on the Knacker's Yard (no longer called Knacker's Yard) where Spillner, the dried-up Onion-head—it was his turn now—unveiled the plaque. Meanwhile it had grown so dark that only the beam of a flashlight saved the situation. The cone of light groped its way up the wall and paused where the words could be read: BALTHASAR KEMPFF—A SON OF OUR CITY. Unobserved, Blumentritt escaped before anyone could draw him into conversation; he came to himself once more at his desk, head propped on his hands. Now secure walls were around him again (comparatively secure), thick walls and his books. If only he were allowed to keep these walls, these bookshelves, he was almost inclined to put up with the lamp post. But no more of these trapeze acts. All he wanted was to be left alone.

He sat there without knowing whether or not he had destroyed himself by that speech—and in whose eyes. How risky dealing with language was, he thought. What came from opening your mouth? Trouble came; you lost the static innocence of children not yet marked by suffering and questionable opinions. What he would have given now to be able to descend once more into the untroubled condition of those who were nothing but a number, a name on an identity card. If only he could sink into the ground, deal with it and be vanquished along with it, and have nothing but his bare living. If only, that is, he could be an unwritten page. To sink out of sight, once more to be nobody—but who could achieve that?

Irregular tinkling of the bell, a fifth up, a fifth down. The sound is so familiar. A battered, splintered frame, the statuette on the shelf, Melanesian, arms akimbo and long noses piled twice above one another, your pets, Blumentritt, the little balancing act. But Frau Zergaden was missing; she was ensconced in Town Hall, has to think of her future, don't blame her for it—or could she possibly have written the anonymous letter? How the thing still preys on your mind—and yet the letter in your breast pocket is half in shreds. Frau Zergaden is gone, "Woman Arising" is gone, Heiland sang her praises in public and promoted her to the cemetery. Now Inez is coming, she has heard the cracked fifths, why doesn't she have the bell repaired? Her negligence, her sloppiness, bothered him, for he was such a lover of order; that was evident from the way he stacked the notebooks on his desk or from his daily habits. He even ran his razor over his cheeks and chin in the same series of strokes each time. But she had not even removed the pedestal on which "Woman Arising" had been standing. And yet she need only push aside the burlap curtain, she need only stand before him, her long legs in motion, her shoulders askew in the jumper she wore, and he wanted to take her into his arms and forget the speech and all the nonsense connected with it. But always, at such times, she had strange bits of news: So-and-so said this about you, and so-and-so said that. Some said: Now he's really burned his tongue nicely with that business about orderly freedom and Saul why persecutest thou me and so on, that sort of thing is sure to turn out badly, he'd better cut the corner—that was the phrase for clearing out—before they took his identity card away, because after all that kind of talk was—they were proud, proud of him again. At last someone had come along who didn't pour out the regular platitudes, and a speech like that gave a person strength for a whole year, it had been a real satisfaction, that's what. And the others said: So this fellow Blumentritt has also given up and gone over to them and knocked the count and turned the life of an

utterly religious man and artist into another version of
the fight for peace, we know that song and dance, next
comes the *Internationale*, and this teacher Blumentritt
wants to have a place among the bigwigs too, that's the
way it is, everyone goes downhill, sooner or later it infects
everyone, they all get ambition and then they forget completely what they've seen for themselves, and wasn't this
Blumentritt another of those resistance fighters or maybe a
deserter who stabbed us all in the back? Anyhow he was
never a real soldier, that we know for certain, and you can
expect anything of that kind, those intellectuals are more
dangerous than the others, at least you can see what you
have to expect from the others, but the intellectuals always
have a few little surprises up their sleeves, and Blumentritt
too has forgotten where he comes from, what a decent
guy his father was, though.

That's your thanks for it, Inez said, and he did not even
have the chance to say Issi to her and to draw her behind
the burlap curtain where she sometimes would forget
about tending the shop for a little or a least let him lean
against her; she knew, after all, how he was starved for all
that; but good Lord, this time, instead, there were her
widening eyes, so innocent, when he asked what her
father thought. Her father? She only looked away and
curled her lips. Odd that she hated her father, here, where
everyone was supposed to love one another (as he had
once told her). The only explanation he could think of
was that she still, to this day, blamed her father for having

pressed her to marry Benjamin Keil. Incidentally, marriage: she was forever dropping the word. Was that
honest? He, Blumentritt, did not insist on it; they more or
less lived together, and that sufficed. Then suddenly she
said: Onion-head has disappeared! What do you say to
that? Why, what should he say to that; one more gone;
the last to go will take the keys, as the popular phrase
went. But what could have been his reason? He wouldn't
be likely to find another such quiet post as that museum
job; he wasn't the kind of man who was sought after on
the other side. Certainly not, she said. Oh rot, he said.
What do we know, she said. And after all, that was Spillner's worry; what did it matter to either of them. But
what, by the way, had happened to her car? Had she received a replacement for it? She only waved that question
aside. Let everything take its course, she said; she certainly
wasn't going to make a fuss; she'd be compensated one
way or another. Odd, he thought, perhaps it may even
work out that way. He kissed her hastily and left for
school, for it was early morning.

During the first recess the principal surprised him by
handing him a form. Nothing special. But he commented:
Here, this column on religion, you certainly don't mean
to fill it out again in the old way. In the old way? Blumentritt asked caustically; would he kindly explain what he
meant. But the principal loved circumlocution; he said
he hoped it would not be necessary for him to remind
Blumentritt of the science of all sciences, from which

certain conclusions might be drawn as to whether or not religion was acceptable nowadays. Blumentritt would understand: one of these days a good deal would be asked of every teacher and therefore of him. Blumentritt left the principal without replying, and went back to his class.

But in the middle of the lesson the janitor comes in, beckons to me, whispers; the class grows restive behind us. I turn around and order: All right now, sum up the progress that has been made. Or something of the sort; we had just been talking about some development; everything develops. And then I followed the janitor. I don't like being called away from lessons; I know these interruptions during classes: "actions," hastily called meetings, a new situation after the latest decrees, new developments. But it was nothing of the sort; this time there was no committee sitting in the faculty room, waiting for me, who am always the last to arrive. It was just the telephone. A telephone call! I answer, press the black earphone against my ear, do not understand at once. Who? Herr Gutsmuts, I don't know any Herr Gutsmuts, not at the Town Hall either where he is calling from and where I am to come for a talk after classes. Do you have time after classes? I am asked, and of course I have time; I can put off my lunch, the way home is not very far, just a hundred steps, the Town Hall is practically at my door. Perhaps he is an

(145

employee of the mayor's office who is to inform me that the town was not satisfied with my speech and I am to deliver another speech making up for the inadequacies of the first. Or else he will tell me that I spoke well, that I am an excellent speaker, and therefore must talk more often. In short, if it has anything to do with the speech, it bodes ill. Or is this going to be about that blank for religion? Well, there I am firm; if they are going to make an issue out of scratching out two letters of the alphabet, I cannot accede, even though one has to admit that two little letters don't mean much, certainly less than a speech, why fuss about them? Or on the other hand would it be the third cock's crow, you have denied me thrice; is that what you went over the horse for? Lashed twenty-five times, congealed to a tiny point, that was how it was, a knot of lava-pain, *wer hat dich, du schöner Wald*, God protect you, I survived it, didn't croak, good luck, so why be worked up about a telephone call: I'll go on living, that's enough, and don't worry, the two letters on my questionnaire will stand.

I stop taking the telephone call as especially portentous; nevertheless it continues to haunt the remaining hours of the morning. I have to think about it continually; it is a great strain to concentrate on the lessons. I give assignments, I let the pupils work alone; they know how to do that, only they aren't used to it from me. They rattle the inkwells; a subdued drumming of victory begins, a quiet, triumphant roll of drums which accompanies my defeat.

Losing my concentration is equivalent to defeat. Gradually noon approaches; the noon hour is drummed in; the notebooks are clapped shut and handed in: What do we know about the basic types of rural settlements? Explain the difference between the nucleated village and the street village. What was the significance of the city wall in the Middle Ages? (I asked this question casually, negligently, thoughtlessly; I should have asked what was its significance for the ruling class.) Does Schochern have a city wall? All the pupils eagerly fall upon this topic.

Schochern! Of course Schochern has a city wall, but Schochern is more than an accumulation of streets and inhabitants, more than a town full of mummified medievalisms, or a pattern of life. Schochern as a prototypal community which breeds faces which close and open, tolerate and reject, without clear reason. A speech, an assignment, a telephone call, may draw you in or shut out; you are praised or walk in solitude across a shadow stage. At the same time I am incapable of concealing myself; my gait identifies me; everyone knows the lame teacher. Blame or fame, that depends, that changes quickly—what do they think of me? Some admire my courage, when they think of the speech, although it was not courage at all; the others, who perhaps only saw my name mentioned in the newspaper, regard me with suspicion, as though I had abandoned them. Why, for example, does Frau Luja no longer talk to me? Why does the printer Pfannstiel, who still has the flowers on his mind, suddenly lay his hand on my

(147

shoulder when I run into him in town and say: "Remember your father. He was an honorable man." I ask him what he means. "Just that," he answers. "You should always remember your father!" I have become sensitive to overtones, perhaps too sensitive; it is as if people on the street already know about the telephone call, and as though they already know what it means, while I alone do not know.

At the Town Hall gate a man in a leather jacket is waiting. He asks my name; naturally he recognizes me; apparently he knows how I walk and how I look. I follow him up the stairs, past the doorkeeper's box; the man in the leather jacket only nods to the doorkeeper. We are admitted; so I am expected; the whole thing goes forward with the speed of a carefully prepared script, and I doubt that it has to do merely with another speech they want me to give. It has the air of something more official and more important. But what of it. I've been called to the Town Hall; there's nothing unusual about that.

We climb to the second floor, to the third; we have passed by Frau Zergaden's door, passed the woman in violet, and still we go on; we must also climb the third set of stairs. Now we are under the tower, where the rooms already have slanting ceilings and dormer windows. We enter one of these rooms (desk, two armchairs in front of it, a wooden chair behind it, no office paraphernalia, just a brief case on the desk). In front of the desk sits another man. That is Gutsmuts, fair-haired, fat, stocky;

he lays aside the newspaper he has been reading, gives his name, invites me to sit beside him. The man in the leather jacket sits down behind the desk and pushes the brief case, which lies open, in my direction, toward the corner of the desk. "We," he says, apparently including himself and the fair-haired Herr Gutsmuts, "are temporarily here in the Town Hall, the headquarters of the municipal government"—and now he looks around the room, so that evidently his "we" includes the three of us. "But we," he continues, and this time he means only himself and Herr Gutsmuts, "we *are from the* . . ."

I cannot say the word. That is the shrill doorbell that calls us away, the word in whose flesh-and-blood reality I have never quite been willing to believe, which has remained inconceivable to me. I have always thought myself safe, safe *from that*. But apparently everyone believes in this fine fiction of invulnerability until it happens to himself, until that happens which refutes all safety, until the words are spoken: "We are from the . . ."

For a brief moment it still seems possible to me that it can all be retracted, that it was only a joke, though a bitter one; nothing has happened, we were only having fun. But a rapid flashing of identifications follows the man's statement that they are from the . . . I will not use the word. Everyone knows that this institution exists; nobody talks about it, for anyone who has anything to do with it prefers to remain invisible, or at any rate to keep mute. Now you must take your stand or refuse to talk, and the one course is as bad as the other; either alternative binds you all the more tightly to this institution. Speaking stimulates its inquisitiveness; silence increases its anger. Try and see whether you can get out of it. So Melzer was right after all. (Melzer who left, his laughter following him. No more Chopin preludes; the king sobs; a rippling of the keys, a trill; Melzer, what's wrong with us!)

"Herr Blumentritt, we are from the . . ."

Nothing, nothing can be retracted now; my name has been spoken, so there is no mistake. My spine feels peculiar; my throat moves oddly on the vertebrae. I smile. It is always best to smile at first. The decision has been made, and nevertheless there is a smile inside me, just in case.

"We have only a few questions on our minds," they say. "You are causing a good deal of talk right now, and therefore we are turning to you with the request for certain information. As far as education goes, we are only bloody laymen compared to you." They say *bloody*. "You can help us."

"How would I be able to help?" I ask in the tone of a sophisticated but modest man. And now they try to convince me of how much I know. Gutsmuts takes the floor, and the more I disparage my own expertise, the more examples he gives which betray how much he himself knows. About guidelines for promotions, for example. To what extent the teacher is to blame for his pupils' failures. Must the curriculum be adhered to precisely, and how precise is precise. (Naturally I know that.) What difficulties in teaching arise out of such restrictions. . . . I say this and that, and all the time I know that they are certainly not concerned about these matters. They want me to mention cases; they name names of teachers and pupils. What is this leading to? Are they on a particular track? Will the name of Kumtsiel be mentioned in a moment?

"You'd do better to ask the school board. Ask them to show you the guidelines—that will be much simpler for you," I say.

"The school board is not sufficiently unbiased."

That is their answer, and now the man behind the desk speaks. Each time the man behind the desk asks something which demands my full attention, Gutsmuts (or the one who calls himself Gutsmuts) confuses me by hurling a dozen names at me from the side. He observes my reactions; but if I turn swiftly to the right, if I take him up and ask: "Are you particularly interested in that name," he quickly evades me, drops that name, and mentions another. I can no longer make any pattern out of the names; the maze has closed behind me.

"What attitude do these pupils have toward the subjects of instruction? Wasn't there an incident in local studies?"

"Not that I recall."

"Do you talk about the history of the town?"

"Rarely."

"Are there others who know the subject better?"

"Possibly," I say, and again I do not know whether

they are referring to Meiran, or to Spillner. I mean to be on my guard against mentioning any names.

"But other views of the subject?" they say.

"I don't know." Are they referring to my speech? Is that what they are really driving at?

"Do the pupils accept everything you say? I hear you have some real delinquents in the school."

"They don't seem that bad to me."

"Still and all, they set fire to posters!"

"I find that hard to believe," I reply, for if I admit it, then I must certainly have some idea of who was responsible.

"Who were the ones again. . . . Keil? Fenk? Schunke?" I no longer react to names, and so they continue: "How old would the culprits be, older than these?"

"Certainly older," I say, and this is already too much, I should pretend to know nothing whatsoever, but it's not always possible to put that across. "The investigation will surely discover that."

All this is still a preliminary skirmish, and I do not even know whether I ought to stand up and go; but anything of that sort angers them; I've heard that from Melzer. What has brought me to this place? Inez, Meiran, Spillner? Is it about the lamp post? (That pleases the enemy, Heiland said.) It is Kumtsiel? The speech? Or the anonymous letter? Did they send it to me, by any chance? They? The letter! I'm still carrying it around in my pocket, but now I can no longer produce it; it's too late. I've neglected to

hand it in, and if they know about it, they know a good
deal about me.

Who does most for the city? they ask. On what terms
am I with the mayor? Is he popular? What do I think of
him, what is the general opinion?

No, I won't say, that is beyond my competence, and I
must even weigh, restrain, phrase carefully the words in
which I refuse information; for now the purpose of the
opened brief case becomes apparent; the man pushes it a
little closer to me and neither of the two men is taking
notes; the brief case does that for them. (I've already
heard a good deal about these things.) Neither Gutsmuts
nor the pale man who has not removed his leather coat
so much as holds a pencil in his hand. I have described
them reasonably enough: fair-haired and pale, Gutsmuts
with the face of a steer. Probably they picked the name
Gutsmuts out of a telephone book. They are blank faces;
an hour after parting I would scarcely be able to identify
them. I'm sorry to say it, but they confirm the general
idea that everyone has of them, confirm it in a farcical
and incredible manner. They seem to be mechanical prod-
ucts, mechanized like the interior of the brief case in
which questions and answers and all subsidiary noises are
preserved. I cough a little into the brief case.

"Posters," Gutsmuts asked, "seem to elicit little affection from intellectual people, I take it?"

"What do you mean by affection?" I evade. But now I
must make a concession to them; from answer to answer I

sound less and less credible if I divorce myself completely from my habit of cautious criticism—of which they know. And so I add: "Of course the posters can't be called handsome, and their frequency defeats their purpose; everything becomes worn out in time. One can't blame a person for not being fond of them."

I feel much relieved after having given this reply; my chest inflates, I feel altogether unembarrassed, I smile again (anyhow, everything has already been decided). The impression I want to give the men is that my conscience is perfectly clear, that I am their critical but friendly adviser. But immediately they come down hard on my friendliness.

"And how is this dislike expressed? Describe it."

I pale, so it seems to me. I try to understand, but even understanding can lead me astray. Did I not once refuse to carry a poster that the pupils tried to force on me?

"I'm not aware that it has been expressed."

"Come now, you as a pedagogue surely see deeper! You have a good relationship to your fellow men and understand their thinking."

What an irony! I really no longer know what they are referring to. My relationship to Heiland? To the authorities? To the enemy? Even Meiran is an enemy. Or do they wish to warn me, who am habitually so solitary, against ties with my fellow men, with whom I have scarcely any ties? Even Frau Luja shuns me. Should I say something about my bad relationship to the authorities?

"Kumtsiel!" the name rings in my right ear.

"I scarcely knew him."

"You associate with Archivist Meiran?"

Associate! What are they getting at now? I offer as harmless an explanation as possible: "He knows a good deal about Balthasar Kempff. Therefore I went to Meiran for certain books and documents that I needed for my festival oration. . . ." Now it has come out; I have done them the favor of presenting my most vulnerable side. I offer them my whole flank. Will they attack there, glad that I have readily fallen in with the game they are playing? But instead they ask about Spillner, Meiran's successor, Onion-head. I really have nothing at all to say about him. I say so a shade too sincerely, too emphatically; I shake my head, shrug my shoulders. Up to this point I have made no such decisive asseverations—another mistake! My emphatic tone diminishes the weight of all my previous answers and makes them dubious, for now they know that this is the first time I have spoken honestly, that I really don't know a thing about Spillner. And they will not find out anything from me about all the others. Oh God, what a miserable chess game, with provocation, loss of pawns, bishop traps! They offer an open game; I advance and am lost. What should I really say to this pale, unhappy man whose duty it is to make others unhappy? I do not even despise him—he is too pale. And the other? But I must not feel any sympathy for them, although their task is not easy. I would be glad to make

(155

the task pleasanter for them, would be ready to help them weave their net, if only I would not catch myself in it. If I had the slightest idea of what they are aiming at, what they wish to arrive at—but that is just what they are not allowed to betray; to do so would destroy their whole plan of campaign. What kind of report would they then have to send on up to their superiors! And so I must not wish them easier work. Let them be more successful with others, but I can't do them a single favor, or the brief case which is recording every word.

"With whom do you usually go to the soccer games?" they ask. But that must be a mistake; I don't go to soccer games. They ask: "Has anyone criticized the slaughter-house plan in your presence?" But I know nothing about any slaughterhouse plan! "Don't try to tell us that," they reply, and there must be something behind that too. "But you are on good terms with the Church?" I don't go to church at all, I reply, but perhaps they are alluding to the fact that the minister sat beside me during the Kempff memorial meeting. Did someone observe the minister's pressing my hand after the speech? "Has anyone been putting pressure on you?" is the next question. Is this the moment to complain? What they want to hear is obscure. Am I to say yes or no? If they are referring to this in-terrogation, I would have to say no, not to offend them, and if they mean the anonymous letter. . . . But it is un-thinkable that they know about that.

"By the way," they suddenly ask, "isn't this man Meiran related to Frau Keil?"

I turn my head quickly to the side from which the question came. "Why does that interest you?"

Already other names are being mentioned; I know some and don't know others; I deny, evade, and even at that say too much. And then—I do not even know whether the most important matter has or has not yet been touched on—in fact, I am convinced that they have avoided asking about whatever is most important to them—then I at last tell them how undignified this conversation seems to me! I do not feel that I can continue to answer their questions, I say. And Herr Gutsmuts (or whatever his real name is) remarks:

"But it was going very well, wasn't it?"

What does that mean, it was going very well! If that were so, I would be greatly upset. Besides, I did not come here to practice a game so that it would go better the next time.

"I don't understand you."

"Our conversation! It certainly doesn't bother you, does it?"

"I have nothing to conceal," I declare emphatically; but they have long ago stopped believing me, and we stand up (I am averse to including the two of them and myself in this "we")—I stand up and they do so likewise, and virtually on the way out the one in the leather jacket says:

"You haven't far to go to reach home. It seems that you're not satisfied with your apartment?"

"It's a roomy apartment," I reply, "but the municipal

radio bothers me at times. It's too loud by day—you can hear that yourself." I turn, raise my arms, and smile as though this were not an interrogation, but a simple appointment. "Besides, the traffic, the parades, the carousel, the shooting gallery: *Step up! Take your turn!* Sometimes it isn't easy to . . ."

I say not a word about the gallows. I don't mention the lamp post, although it has brought all this down on my head. Or am I mistaken? A ludicrous story, but if I had not insisted on seeing Heiland, perhaps I would have been spared all these vexations. No one would have asked me to make that speech, no telephone call would have summoned me, summoned me here and possibly to an entirely different place. . . . Or would it—nevertheless? And still I go on saying to myself: What are you guilty of, that they confer upon you the wretched honor and the miserable distinction of this institution which makes a spy out of you, so that you can no longer look people in the face, so that you are no longer safe even from yourself— have you betrayed yourself or will you betray yourself; the cock crows secretly and there is no way out, or only one way out.

"Are you considering moving to another apartment?" they ask me casually.

"I've decided against it."

"Hardly worth the trouble?" Gutsmuts asks.

They imply that I am planning to skip out. They want me to know that they can read my mind. Do they expect me to redden? But I remain unshaken; I have nothing to admit. What they suspect is far from my thoughts, that is, it was, up to this moment.

"Aside from the noisiness, it would be hard to find a better apartment," I say. We are still standing; they think I am now relaxed and off my guard. It looks quite like a casual conversation, but it is in fact only the second part of the interrogation, which they have decided to conduct in the atmosphere of parting.

"What do the other residents think about what happens in the square? We'll want to ask you about that, sometime."

"I couldn't tell you; I have no contact with my neighbors."

"But your opinion on these things sets the tone; people know who you are, after all, and express their views to you."

"I live a very retired life."

"You know how to talk to people all right! Didn't you even write something once? We'll leave it at that—we'll be turning to you."

"Then you will hear only my private reactions, which can't be of much use to you."

"By the way, we would recommend"—at this point they flank me, one on either side—"recommend *in your own interest* that you say nothing about this conversation to anyone. We have our means and methods. Believe us, we find out about everything."

"I know." They have conducted me to the stairs; there they take their leave. They are still smiling; so far they confine themselves to warnings. Next time I will have to sign something, like Melzer. But it will not come to that point.

"See you again," they call after me.

But the decision has been taken. Everything that happened to me before this visit to the Town Hall, everything that constituted my life and my daily experiences, has been torn loose, belongs to the past, is over and done with. From the very first words those men spoke, the break was irrevocable; it started with their: *We are from the . . .*

I did not expect that the telephone call would mean that.

He still had a few hours left, one more night before his train departed. He bought the ticket, then returned from the railroad station to town. There was still the matter of packing his suitcase, saying goodbye to Inez—a temporary or a final goodbye. He did not know which; he had not gone to see her yet, so that, if he were being watched, it would not look as if he were taking his secret straight to her. He had already cleared out his apartment and library of anything which might additionally incriminate him (even afterwards, after the irrevocable, he would still be afraid). A few more errands, precautions, and then what? A trapeze artist, even if he had fouled up his star act, left the arena smiling.

And he walked once more through the streets in which he had collected the impressions of his lifetime—everything that stuck came out of his childhood. All images piled up in front of the sluice gate which he had lowered in front of his past; they all continued to live only in memory. Over and done with. Everything broken off. He tried to picture the break; he looked at everything as if he had already lost it all. He came to that place beneath the bridge where his father, bent over wood and glue, had passed his years in work. Strangely, his father emerged out of the past more vividly than anything else. Only now, it seemed to him, was he finally bidding farewell to his father. He drew confidence and courage from that memory. He saw his father half turned away, sulkily stooping, a soft, sad line around his mouth, like a rejected child's. He had been a taciturn man, apparently without any deeper understanding of his son—but that, of course, had been illusory. Blumentritt saw that now; it had always been a case of excessive vulnerability hiding behind a mask of apathy and in that they had been similar, he and his father. All along, Blumentritt had repressed the image of his father. Only now was he able to slip inside his father's skin and begin to understand him. He even knew why. This was the moment at which his own tendency to static isolation was breaking down, his inclination to shut himself up behind walls (that was how he saw his father, isolated; that was how he understood himself now, at this moment when his task was to overcome his static nature). All this was memory; not even the house still stood. Yet he saw it, the porch, the workshop, the small, crammed rooms, the dark hallway, the stairwell, the statue of the watchman holding the lantern. Everything else paled by comparison. And it seemed to Blumentritt as though his whole life had taken place between this house on the Wilm and his apartment on the Fish Market.

Blumentritt turned away, walked for some distance along the Wilm, then uphill along narrow streets. He remembered the black princess, remembered what it was to have a boy's body, the play on the stage, the Chopin prelude, Melzer trilling and Grandfather Metzeki your children eat a lot—then he turned in the direction of the cemetery. Why so? He did not want to visit any graves. He only recalled that he had walked this way across the whole town up to the cemetery, from the Fairy Fountain on the other side of the river by way of the Boulevard of Progress and the Bridge of Friendship down the Avenue of Peace and up the mountain—had walked this way not so very long ago, following the crowd, when the great friend of all peoples, the supreme chief with the two-syllabled name, had died: Blumentritt, cap in hand, filing with slow steps across the Fish Market to the strains of the Funeral March—Chopin?—of many funeral marches past the platform for the military officers and officials who stood representing the dead man, hands on the visors of their caps, receiving the honors. Then the parade up the mountain to the bust of the greatest man of all times (so the newspapers wrote), to the monument in the cemetery, Kummerbart's bust, the last of his works. For seven hours Blumentritt had marched and stood bareheaded; a violent cold was the last benefit conferred on him by the ruler with the two-syllabled name who a few years after his death would no longer be hailed as the great humanitarian. They had made a pilgrimage to him, Blumentritt and the other teachers; but now he swerved off that path. He climbed up to the castle instead of the cemetery. The way was steep. Blumentritt walked too fast; he panted for breath. He came to the entrance to the vault. It was closed. Too bad, he would have liked to see bones just now, real bones of real dead men who chuckled at night and rattled around inside the vault. Instead he found a yellowed sign beside the door: The vault may be inspected by appointment. Museum Director Meiran. The name had been crossed out. Above it was written: Spillner. That name too was crossed out. It was really too bad; he no longer had time to make an appointment to see the vault, and he would not have known with whom to make it.

Walking downhill was easier. At the door of his place he noticed that the doorknob squeaked as it turned; he imagined that this squeaking would remain in his memory. The upper part of the door consisted of tall panes of milk glass with a pattern of stippled flowers. For a long time he stood in front of Frau Luja's wardrobe, the mirror of which he sometimes used while he combed his hair. Frau Luja crept soft-footed through the apartment as though there were a corpse in the house. She switched on the hall light. Her cheeks were slightly flushed just under her eyes.

"You're not going to be leaving us?" she asked, pressing two fists against her chin.

"What gives you that idea? I'm taking a trip—nothing unusual about that."

"And what about your things? What will you want to take along? I haven't any idea what you mean by a trip."

Had she noticed anything? Had she been in his rooms during his absence? So far, he had prepared only a brief case with his most important papers; the suitcase still lay on a chair, empty. He could understand Frau Luja's uneasiness; after all, he did not take trips very often, never outside the regular school vacations. He had little enough experience in traveling, and that not very satisfactory: moving back and forth, not very far in one direction and not very far in the other; a temporary feeling of being liberated from everything, and a hangover afterwards, a dull sensation of having been cheated—flying out to the end of a string and being pulled back again. Once he had gone with a small group of delegates to a memorial meeting at the concentration camp. That had been a mistake also. They walked back and forth among the foundations of the stone barracks. Behind him someone said: Here is where I lay! But there was no telling whether the man meant during or after the war; he spoke very softly. Had he been a man like Blumentritt or like Grünmeissel? Nothing had changed; everything confirmed Heiland's phrase: Who—whom! (And it was not even Heiland's own phrase.)

"Don't worry, Frau Luja. I'm not going to need more than this single suitcase."

"And what about—what about your laundry? And the rent?" She remembered that just in time.

"Why don't I pay that right now, in advance." He could not offer her more than the next month's rent; that would only have made her more suspicious. "A sudden summons," he said. "Nothing I could have anticipated."

She crossed her arms over her chest and looked past him. He did not dare to speak openly with her; they were not that intimate. Besides, he did not want to endanger her. And then, she had spied on him, to a certain extent.

Blumentritt shook hands with her. "Many thanks," he said. "I'm touched, the way you take care of me. I could never find a better landlady."

He flushed and went into his room. He did not want to waste any more time, did not want to wait until the following morning and steal away out of his warm bed. He thought to make use of the evening, to take his suitcase to the baggage room in the station, and then to spend the night with Inez. It would be easier running away from a strange house—harder to leave her, of course, but he would have to steel himself for that.

Packing the suitcase was almost too much for him. All at once he grasped the undetermined value of objects. What should he take with him? To put on your coat suddenly and part with the photo on your desk: the picture of a man at a desk on whose desk stood the picture of a man at a desk on which again a picture could be seen. . . . He let all that stand. The thought of having forgotten something vital obsessed him: an identification, a letter, a document. He packed very little and closed the suitcase. He had on his gray, rather threadbare coat over his best suit, contemplated the hat he had never worn on the clothes hook (he never cared for hats), picked up a ballpoint pen, a pencil, a fountain pen, and then he remembered the books—volumes purchased second hand, in dirty gray cloth bindings, with dozens of memoranda slips tucked into the pages. He put three of the books into his suitcase.

When he left the room, Frau Luja was standing outside. "Everything's all right," he said hastily, brushing by her with his suitcase and brief case. "I'll leave the room unlocked. Goodbye—I'll be back soon." He bumped into the hall door; it opened violently, quivering on its hinges. Frau Luja stared after him, her hands pressed against the arteries of her throat. Cane tucked under his arm, he limped downstairs. At the front door it occurred to him that he had forgotten the Luminal tablets. He left his baggage and stole back to the apartment once more. When he left at last, he felt as if he had committed a successful burglary in a stranger's home.

In doubt, hope, and fear, he thought of next morning and the end of the following day. By then it would all be behind him. He deposited his suitcase and brief case at the checkroom in the railroad station. On the way back into town, he told himself: this anxiety is nothing unusual; on the contrary, I would feel very strange without all this uncertainty. You gradually become accustomed to it as you do to an animal gnawing inside walls, or to a cat skulking around the door, which you've vainly chased away several times—until you realize that you would miss it some day if it did not turn up. He began to fear that he would miss something once he departed, something he could not precisely define, a feeling more than anything else. How should he put it: insecurity, spying on himself? How far could he go in expressing this? Being pledged to the rules of caution. Suspicion like a mountain which everyone was digging into in the effort to find each other. He would lose a certain tension, and he did not know with what it could be replaced. With memory? Self-assurance? No amount of concentration upon oneself was as reliable as enforced watchfulness. And perhaps he was purchasing liberation from the thing that oppressed him at the cost of lowering his strength.

At any rate, Blumentritt would be leaving without hatred. What he could not fathom was why people

were forever tormenting each other on earth, at the in-
stigation of some obscure impulse. Why wouldn't they
let each other alone? He would never fully comprehend
it. Never.

Incapable of imagining that this was to be the last time,
overpowered by an alarming indifference, he set out for
Crooked Hill—never mind what it was called nowadays.
He would always remember it, of course, as Crooked
Hill; all of childhood (which you never fully outgrow)
—and all the names and nooks and crannies and fairy
tales he remembered wreath crown and head every step
a trembling of the dwarfs he remembered the melody of a
voice of a sound of a moment incidentally or a moon-
beam quivered in the nursery there had been a brawl
down by the river on the shore of the Wilm close by
the reeds lying on his back he looked into the silken
blue sky swept clear of clouds remembered a blue silk
girl's chemise panties he lay in the grass nice hen nice
rooster and you pretty particolored cow, rhythms, Hanfstengel and Melzer trilling and what do you say to that
and smells of tar and tinder an old man a vest full of
buttons and silver badges keep it up boys—there was the
house. The garden gate was closed. He opened it himself and rang although he had all the keys; the people
upstairs did not care who came and who rang. He saw

no light on the lower floor. Inez was not home; her coat was not hanging in the wardrobe. Sometimes she went to see women friends and stayed away overnight. She did not tell him every time she went visiting; he had no telephone. After all, it was no great loss if they missed one another for an evening. But this time everything was different. He had not imagined that his last night in Schochern would be like this; it confused him. When she had not returned after an hour, he grew restive. Slowly, he drifted through the rooms of her apartment. Except for the hall light and a small table lamp, he had put no lights on. Gradually, as he lost all sense of time, he asked himself whether it would not be better if he went away without bidding goodbye to Inez, if he merely left a note for her and vanished at dawn, leaving her free to follow him or not, as she wished. Frau Luja's trivial song choked him: I must go out into the world. He felt weak. No, he would not leave a note; why should be burden her with dangerous knowledge?

In the semidarkness he groped through the apartment, opening one door after the other. Order everywhere, everything picked up. No clothing over the chair in the bedroom, a few items missing from the bathroom—it was clear she would not be coming home tonight.

Blumentritt thought of going to sleep; he must take the early morning train if he wanted to be gone before school opened. For then his absence would be noted. He envisioned the excitement he would be causing. He was suddenly tearing his life in two, jerking the rudder around so brusquely, to the accompaniment of so much public stir. A premonition of the things that would be said about him filled him with uneasiness. Breaking with the world, even with the most irrational of worlds, brought it home to you that there were things for which man was not made. A taint was left behind. Nevertheless, this departure seemed to him far more bearable than a life under the eyes of Herr Gutsmuts, or whatever his name was.

There was no hiding and no escape from Gutsmuts. All at once he felt sick of brooding over the matter. He sat down, still in semidarkness. A man in an airless room. A man in a beach cabin, floating between here and there. He was elsewhere, had already departed; neverthless he was still in the same city in which his apartment was located, to which Frau Luja was expecting him to return (he could go back, this very night). He was only experimentally elsewhere, beyond the divide. The notion roused in him a vehement urge to action. Various measures sprang to mind, letters he might write, applications he might draw up, questionnaires he would have to fill out. But the time for all that had not yet come. He limped through the apartment. Too many things were rushing at him. He needed relaxation, space, air, movement.

No hope of going to sleep. He left the house and tramped back and forth in the street outside, avoiding the circle of light cast by the street lamp. Crossing the street, he slunk along the fence there. A milky veil of mist had descended. The thin spot of light from the lamp post hovered above it. Blumentritt reached Heiland's house. Its outlines glimmered through the mist. Suppose he went in and confessed everything to Heiland! The temptation was suddenly overwhelming, positively voluptuous. It was the challenge of danger. One dialogue and he was done for. How odd that was; you lived by formulas, pronounced the proper formula and survived. Heiland had always known how to do that consummately well. And so he came out on top, charged others with mistakes which he too had committed, reprimanded harshness when it was no longer time for harshness, let others fall while he himself held on. He knew what was wanted of him. Why couldn't Blumentritt learn to play the game, the game of strategy and correct formulas? By now, it was so absurd that often he could laugh at it, and at other times was irritated to tears; often he only shook his head in scorn at it all, while at other times it reduced him to uncomprehending sadness. One thing he knew for certain: to go to Heiland and speak openly would be the end. For that was breaching the commandment: Thou shalt keep thy mouth shut. The milky night mist, dropping in veils over Crooked Hill, surrounded him, cut off his view as soon as he turned away from the circle of light from the street lamp. He saw shadows, was himself only a shadow; he closed his eyes, his stiff leg blundered into a pile of earth, he stumbled, and as he caught himself, someone's breathing, someone's voice struck him. "What are you doing here?"

Heiland stood before him, laughing; his teeth flashed out of the darkness. A patch of light no bigger than a fist illuminated his glasses, nose, mouth, and chin. Heiland must have come down a side street and approached the cone of light which was set down like a bucket over Blumentritt, so that he was seen but saw nothing. Now, however, he made out Heiland's whole figure. "Were you ringing next door, and getting no answer?" Heiland asked. "Come in for a few minutes, and rest." Blumentritt heard at his side the hissing noise Heiland made while breathing.

Heiland half pushed him across the street to the garden gate. "Come along, we'll have a cup of tea together." Blumentritt could no longer escape; he must pull himself together now. To spend his last evening with Heiland— the coincidence of it hypnotized him. Already he was entering the house, which seemed a perfect duplicate of the house next door. The floor plan was exactly the same; only the furnishings made everything strange: the carved desk in Heiland's living room, the piano along the wall, the two leather-covered armchairs and the dark, high-backed chairs. They were ranged in exact order around the heavy table. All the furniture seemed curiously taller than that in Inez's house, and the rooms lower. Blumentritt observed the embroidered throw on the piano and the photographs on display upon it. Yet these rooms lacked all signs of a home atmosphere; the

bookshelves with their volumes in blue and brown arti-
ficial leather bindings looked as commercial as an office.

"Where were you bound for?" Heiland asked, as he
took cups and glasses from a china closet. "Can't you get
any rest even at night?"

"Oh yes," Blumentritt replied. "It's not especially late,
you know. You too seem to have felt the need for a walk."

"Yes, a good stimulus to the mind." Heiland was still
holding the second brandy glass in his hand. "At night,
when everything is quiet, one considers what—good Lord,
I almost offered you the glass with my kidney stone!
Would you care to see it? This is the kidney stone I once
passed."

"Ah—hm."

"Pardon me, better take this other glass. What was I
about to say?"

"Greetings to God," a tinny voice sounded from the
adjoining room. There followed a shrill cawing.

"One considers what one can do to get the people
to . . ." But again he did not finish the sentence; he went
into the kitchen and put water on to boil. Then he returned. "To get the people to—how does the phrase go?
One step backward, two steps forward, you understand?
That's how the textbooks put it."

"Two steps forward, one step backward, I think."

"I see you are well informed. One considers, then, what
to do to win over the people. I really don't know, of
course, but I suppose that still has to be done." And as

he brought the tea he continued: "Every so often people need encouragement to go on with the struggle. We ourselves are overcome by lassitude at times. I suppose that's because man is still imperfect; otherwise he would advance faster."

"Man also lives by feelings," Blumentritt replied. "He experiences doubt, restiveness, sorrow. All that is part of him."

"So it's said." Heiland smiled. "Is that an excuse: Feelings must come from somewhere, perhaps from the environment. Perhaps it's the fault of this damned old-fashioned town, this medievalism; people should extirpate those feelings, but they don't."

"Bring me the cassock," the tinny voice in the adjoining room called.

"Later," Heiland answered. He filled the brandy glasses. Perhaps he had an insane housekeeper; who else could it be? "Let's have a drink!"

Blumentritt let the glass stand and asked: "Who's that, talking in there?"

Heiland smiled. "A parrot," he explained. "My only company when I sit over my textbooks at night. An inheritance from my predecessor in this house, a crazy and not altogether kosher clergyman. I suppose you knew about him. He taught the parrot all sorts of nonsense. I've been able to cure it of some, but not all the weird things it says."

"Doesn't it bother you?"

"It amuses me," Heiland replied. He downed a second glass of brandy. "All the same, it should be possible to educate the bird out of some of these superstitions. 'Be ye cheerful in hopes,' it sometimes says, and that's not bad." Heiland produced some rattling sounds as he laughed. He drank a third glass and suddenly forgot to laugh. "Why are these Christians so gay?" he said. "They don't have much to laugh about, with their gloomy religion and those dried-up preachers who keep hell warm for them. Have you ever figured it out?"

"To an extent," Blumentritt said cautiously. "They have something they're certain about; they're already saved before they suffer. You, on the other hand—" he quickly corrected himself. "We, on the other hand, are dependent upon what we are able to promise ourselves. Our faith in the future is, you know, always limited by our own human inadequacies."

"I didn't mean that at all!" Heiland countered. "We can accomplish anything. If we don't squander our strength on incidentals, we will be able to overcome every handicap. But if we constantly let our feelings—"

"But you said that you too—"

"That is something else again." Once more Heiland drank. The man's continual, hasty drinking embarrassed Blumentritt; he too emptied his glass. "That's something else again," Heiland repeated, rather hoarsely. "I rationalize that immediately. One step backward, two steps forward. I'll tell you about that shortly."

"Is that why you asked me in?" Blumentritt wondered at the man's strange need to communicate. He shut his ears to the occasional sallies from the parrot ("Great God, we praise Thee"), and tried to ignore the rattling sound which accompanied Heiland's breathing and which grew worse the more Heiland drank. Blumentritt returned to the subject: "You underestimate man's dependence on his feelings!"

"Ho!" Heiland bared his teeth, but no laughter emerged. "Are you referring to yourself?"

"Myself?"

"What did you gain by your repeated petitions to the town government? Nothing!"

"What does that prove?" Blumentritt asked.

"To us, only usefulness matters. And if I were to put myself in your position for a moment"—Heiland seemed, to judge by the uncertain, waving gestures of his hand, to be falling more and more under the influence of the alcohol—"I would have to say, with utmost objectivity: Your feelings only get you into difficulties."

"I cannot imagine what difficulties you mean." Of course he knew quite well—but did he know everything?

Heiland leaned back, lowered his eyes, delivered himself of what he had to say with scarcely a movement of his yellow teeth. At the same time this posture made him more human. "You don't have to put on any act. Do you—really—fail to see—what is at stake?" He repeated once more, rapidly: Doyoureallyfailtoseewhatisatstake?"

Over the neck of the bottle he fixed his gaze upon Blumentritt. "All that fuss of yours about the lamp post has got
you involved in an affair which you take completely out
of context and examine in and for itself. That's inadmis-
sible. Don't you agree? It might even appear that you
were pursuing a different, cunning purpose and that your
complaints were only a stratagem, only a beginning. You
put the whole thing in the form of a suggestion; the
truth of the matter is, you are getting at something else
entirely—"

"That is an accusation," Blumentritt said. "You're not
just hypothesizing something, you are accusing me."

"Yes, I am doing that. Is that the reason I'm so unpopular with the people? Well, I imagine that situation will
change. You'll see." He made a pause while he drank. "I
may as well tell you right now that your affair has taken
an unfortunate turn. And now, of course, you will ask:
Why is he telling me all this?" He did not want answers;
he always supplied the answers himself. Heiland practiced
the game of self-posed questions which his able tutors,
who stood in long rows on the bookshelves, had developed
to a fine art. "Why do I speak of this? We know some
very careful people who one day get involved in some
private issue, or they have some hobby or other, some pet
peeve, let's say, that becomes a kind of obsession. It
may be in the field of radio programs or onion exports or
the color of uniforms! That's how it starts, doesn't it?
They criticize a detail—and mean the system. Or at the

beginning they haven't reached that point; they mean their criticisms in good faith, they just wish our people had more onions and are all cut up that they don't. They consider that sort of thing positive criticism; they think they can afford it, and for a while all goes well. But not forever. They shouldn't stretch their credit that way. Because one day a little twist takes place, and the reactionary character of the hobbyhorse comes out into the open. You, too, consider your personal concerns as unimportant, but who knows, maybe one of these days even you will be tripped up."

"I don't know how—"

"Of course. You think it's all unimportant. But let us look at it in context." Heiland filled his glass. He drank; he was breathing rapidly. "Perhaps you carry your criticism, your annoyance, into school with you. I'm only giving an example! You might, let's say, refuse to carry a poster in a parade. And why not? Or else you don't decorate your windows. Or you simply leave the demonstration."

"That is grotesque," Blumentritt replied. "You know I'm not well, that I have a physical disability—"

"Why are you getting excited? I was only giving an example, but you admit that it was so! Go on."

"My physical and nervous ailment—I don't like to talk about it, believe me. And if it happens to prevent me from doing one thing or another, that has nothing to do with my political position."

"But in the past you always went along! You never left a demonstration before."

"Then that was my mistake," Blumentritt said.

"Exactly."

"I don't happen to like to refer to my illness; it's embarrassing to me to have to use it as an excuse."

"As I said," Heiland bent over his glass, brought it to his lips, and with a jerk of his head downed the drink; he swelled, looked as if he were already floating above his chair. "As I said, a ridiculous affair, seems at first not worth mentioning. But if it is seen in the context of the lamp-post business, and one must see everything in context, then the arguments take on a good deal more weight."

"What arguments? In regard to what?" Blumentritt waited patiently.

"In the first place," Heiland began, "the town council had already considered the question of new street lights and had decided that they were to be postponed in favor of the slaughterhouse. The slaughterhouse was more important. All that discussion is some time back. We therefore ask: Did you know that? Yes, you must have known it. Therefore, your sham arguments only concealed your aim to criticize this decision. In the second place, a former town council had deliberately postponed the building of this slaughterhouse and wasted the money on a skating rink which is not yet finished. In doing so, it deliberately sabotaged our food supplies. I don't mean to assert bluntly

that you belong to this group, but perhaps you sympa-
thize with it. Your criticism points in the same direction,
or else you wanted to divert the attention of the populace
to a subsidiary question, and that at a moment when all
forces are . . ."

"There is always a moment when all forces are . . ."
Blumentritt interrupted. But he did not accept the verdict
which was being driven home in so passionate, infuriating
a way. It was all too absurd, and he asked: "Are you serious about this? Do you really believe it?"

"No." Silence. Then Heiland said: "Let us leave that
aside for the moment."

He said no. I, Blumentritt, heard him say no. And I
quickly pursued this with: "Then why do you go in for
that kind of reasoning?"

"Because there is a consistent logic to it."

So he does believe it, after all. And if I submit to this
logic, I can almost believe it myself. It's just this trick
of balancing on the border of disbelief and belief which
makes us all so helpless and at the same time so endangers
us. What should I reply to this man who seems to me floating in the room, more and more under tension (from
what? from alcohol?)? His beady eyes are still the same,
his speech is unchanged. His intensity is increasing rather
than diminishing; he is surpassing himself; everything

seems to be merely a charge, etherealized, as though his
body has been reduced to a pencil sketch, as though he
will float through the room with phantom ease, following a line of sight from my eyes, and be projected against
the walls, then vanish and reappear. But he said no! Did
this *no* have any meaning? I must not miss the opportunity to catch him up on that *no*, even if it should be
in vain. "Why are you telling me all this? If the aim is
to trip me up, there is no need to invent this kind of
farce, which you yourself obviously don't believe."

"One must see the connection."

Again the parrot calls out, and for a moment I cannot
separate what the parrot has said and what Heiland has
said.

"There is no connection," I say. "The one thing has
nothing to do with the other."

"Everything exists only in context." I know why
Heiland keeps harping on that. Probably the result of
his evening's reading. Context! Connections! All that is
sheer hollowness, words feeding on words. The enthusiasm, conviction, logic, are all molded to the words.
What should I do? Keep silent? Or should I confess?
What a sweet temptation! What an itch to expose all my
cards and reveal my last treasonable weakness, the interrogation at Town Hall. It seems to me that temporarily
we are equals, but that, too, is an illusion. In reality the
man before me is the voice of the law, or else the floating, ephemeral, phantasmal law itself, open to every in-

terpretation, and from whose glory even exceptions do not subtract one jot or tittle.

"There is no connection," I say.

"You might," Heiland replies, "be peeved by your unsuccessful private battle over the lamp post. That sort of thing makes you incautious. You are depressed by your failure and begin neglecting your social responsibilities. Just for example."

Plausible—only he forgets what part *he* played in that battle. "First you begin at one end, then at another. Which was cause and which the effect?" I ask.

"It comes to the same thing. The one throws light on the other."

"Then there is no defense!" I reply. "If I answer one charge, you present me with another."

What God hath wrought—no, that's the parrot; I won't listen to it any more. It really is too annoying. Heiland's own reply is: "You have worked yourself into a tight corner. That happens to everyone who lets things go so far."

Heiland drinks. He seems to me to be drinking immoderately, but he will not keel over. Meanwhile, I am gradually discerning a framework of connections underlying his words. What does it all mean? You can begin at one end or at the other. To be exact, there is neither end nor beginning; you are always in the midst of the entanglement.

"Am I scanting my responsibilities because of the lamp

post? Or is it my incorrect attitude toward society that leads me into becoming involved in a private battle, as you call it."

Once more the teeth are bared, but Heiland does not answer; he won't commit himself. The facts are known; that suffices; he has already said too much. But what kind of facts are they? When, I ask myself, was suspicion first directed toward me? I shall put this question frankly to him. Why shouldn't I? After all, this is my last night in Schochern. I am practically on my way already. I flash a thought back to my apartment, another ahead of me, and ask: "There must be a beginning to everything; at some time I made myself unpopular. Can't you tell me what that was?"

"The beginning?" Heiland considers. "Unimportant! But as a matter of fact you showed your colors very early."

"Showed my colors early?"

"Perhaps you no longer even recall it. To be plain: it was after a soccer match."

What in the world can he mean? Until the past six months, there were no sinister incidents in my life. I have never attended a soccer match!

Heiland continued: "Perhaps you know no more about soccer than I. I don't even recall the year in which the world championship took place, or whatever it was. What did you think about it?" Heiland asks the question directly, but I am incapable of replying. "A team from

(183

West Germany was playing against a neighbor of ours to the East, a country with which we have friendly relations. Do you remember how you reacted?"

How was I supposed to have reacted!

"While the game was being transmitted over the radio, you and I were at a meeting together. Do you recall? After the meeting was over, we went to a restaurant. To the left—I remember that precisely—to the left of the entrance was the counter. We entered . . ."

And now—now I remember it. A restaurant. A tunnel of a room, the counter right beside the door, the room only moderately filled. That was before the beginning of the afternoon lecture. Some of my fellow teachers were standing around the radio, and if I am not mistaken, Kumtsiel was among them. Kumt was experienced at meetings; he took me under his wing. Moreover, he had a passion for soccer, and I stayed close to him, although soccer games ordinarily did not interest me. At the beginning of the afternoon session we were standing by the radio. Goals were made; the score was two all at halftime. The game was not yet over, and it was high time we returned to the hall for the meeting. Kumt had to tear himself away. When we entered the hall, the meeting had already begun. We sat down in the last row. Every so often Kumtsiel would nudge me and point to his wrist watch, meaning: By now the game is decided! To please him, I pretended that I too was excited over the outcome of the game. The team of the Eastern coun-

try was highly favored; the equal score at half-time had
been a surprise. So the time passed; we lived through the
lecture and then we rushed downstairs to the restaurant,
along with many of our colleagues. Everyone stormed
up to the barman, who stood behind the bar, holding a
mug of beer, enjoying his superior knowledge. Calmly,
he announced: "Beat them three to two!" But who
had been the victor? The Western team! The deciding
goal had come only in the last minutes of play; the barman gave an exact description of it, from halfway over
to the right foul line, so and so many minutes before the
end. He repeated the results, was asked again: Who won?
The Western team! Three to two—then came the name
of the scorer again, the minute, the final result, the scorer's
name. . . . We went over to our table; I don't know
whether Kumtsiel showed how pleased he was, right off.
The others gave no sign, only exchanged looks. We sat
down in silence. The others went on about the lecture,
repeating and expatiating on various points. Evidently
they wanted to conceal their astonishment, their incredulity, or their delight. Then Kumtsiel called to the waiter:
"Let's have two brandies with the coffee!" When the
waiter came, Kumt took the two glasses from the tray
without waiting to be served, and handed me a glass.
Then I knew that he was glad. I was glad with him; it
was nice, our having something that linked us. To the
score! I was infected by the gesture, by its liberating
quality. I raised my glass and drank. "Incredible, isn't it!"

I said. I know I have one weakness: when I receive wholly unexpected, improbable, and remarkable news, I can't help smiling. I tilt my head back and shake it in surprise; this dumb show takes quite a while. That was how I must have behaved, just like that. Kumtsiel put his glass down on the table. We looked at each other. Someone seated opposite us said: "Very interesting."

"And so you simply could not control yourself," Heiland continues. "You must have talked about it at the table, or else your face betrayed undisguised delight at the defeat of our friends!"

"But it's impossible—you can't interpret it that way."

"Isn't it true that you were glad?"

"I don't know a thing about soccer. But Kumtsiel— Kumtsiel!" I burst out spontaneously. "Beg pardon, Kumtsiel has been arrested."

"He has already been released," Heiland replies. "He was convicted, but then he was released. In spite of that, an enemy. Don't you know he said: 'The Saviour also wanted to feed a whole city with three fishes.'* Because he was a party member, we've merely sent him into industry. But we can't let him loose on the youth any more."

Kumtsiel! No doubt Heiland is not revealing every-

---

* An untranslatable pun. *Heiland*=Saviour.

thing they have against Kumtsiel—but how disenchanted Kumtsiel must be. It goes hard with people like him.

"Of course you were glad!" Heiland continues. "It showed all over you. Next day I drove to a meeting with some of the comrades. They were talking about you in the car. Did you notice him yesterday? one of them asked. Yes, the other said; now he's unmasked; we've seen through him now. At least we know where we stand. There you have it, Blumentritt."

You can cook your goose over a soccer game. Is there any refutation? I don't think so. A soccer game, of course; a look of pleasure, and someone saw the look. I understand. One has to control oneself; in the final analysis, there is no excuse. Everyone else controls himself better than I do.

"Why," I ask superfluously, "why must one subscribe to the official view of a soccer game? You smile. Why are you talking with me at all? Why did you ask me to come in?"

How corrupt I must seem to him. He does not even object to my question. Suddenly he is pacing the room. What's wrong with the man? In walking, he shows no sign of drunkenness; he paces back and forth, between piano and desk, looking at the white doilies and the brandy glasses, at the kidney stone. He shows his yellow, close-set teeth as though he has an unpleasant taste in his mouth. But I am mistaken; he is not looking at the doilies at all, but at the photographs. And then he says: "Why do

I go on being concerned about you? Because in a certain way your case touches me closely. For another reason than you may imagine."

"What reason may that be? I can't clear myself to you, even if I should drop the whole lamp-post affair from now on. It's washed too much up to the surface."

"Suppose I only wanted to give you a scare? Because you meddle in things that . . ."

"All the same," I object, "the man they strung up outside my window."

". . . that are really my concern?"

"I don't understand."

"It was my son they hanged."

What's happened? How much more must I strain my senses, how many more words must go through my head, how many more images must haunt my eyes? I experience it once more, and constantly; I see it before me, that final act in the Fish Market. I lay in my room, helpless and shunned, with my bad leg; but my leg had helped me to freedom, had helped me survive in Frau Luja's parlor. My parents had been burned to death in their house by the Wilm. Schochern was not yet occupied. SS men with their death's-head insignia had barricaded themselves in the castle overlooking the city. Artillery fire could be heard in the distance, and then had come that final scene in the Fish Market. A young soldier from an anti-aircraft unit had been led in front of the house by SS military police. He was seventeen or eighteen. Perhaps he had deserted; perhaps he'd only been thinking of the places where he had played as a child, prisoner's base, onesy, twosy, and when the artillery began to boom he thought he had to save himself for the future. Or else he thought nothing at all and ran directly into the arms of the military police. The police had to hold him when the officer pronounced sentence on him. They brought a ladder over from the fruit stand, clambered up on it, threw the rope over the lamp post, and knotted the noose. The condemned boy did not see that; he stood turned away from the lamp post, between the two MP's, who wore a chain, the insignia of their branch of the service, running slantwise across their chests. They brought a chair from the fruit stand and planted it under the noose. When the condemned boy saw the chair, he screamed so horribly that they struck him across his open mouth. He gave them more trouble than they had expected. Cigarettes fell from his pocket. Then, to cut it short, they strung him up.

Did I understand aright? But Heiland has paused in front of the piano. He turns to me and repeats: "He was my son. He was with an anti-aircraft battery near Schochern and probably wanted to dash for home when he saw the Allied troops were coming."

"But—" I try to reply, but find it difficult; I cannot

quite control my voice, must begin again several times and clear my throat. "But why have you never told me that?"

"Because, because we too have—have grown apart. Time has parted us; I don't have much to tell you these days. It isn't my fault, and perhaps not yours either."

"You know," I reply with some bitterness, "I am not one of those who killed your son."

"That may be," he says, "but it doesn't change anything. Still and all, we don't belong together. What do you think is the reason for that?" he asks me like a teacher quizzing a pupil.

"Because you have erected new walls," I reply. My bitterness is deep, partly because I am overcome by sympathy. This man now seems to me deeply pitiable. "We should find it easier to get along with each other. After all, our past might have been a link between us."

"Do you think so? I don't. You forget the class difference."

"Class difference! An abstraction. In that case, you've never been sufficiently humiliated. There are experiences . . ." I am reluctant to speak of my time in camp.

"All that is too many years ago," he says. "People develop along different lines. And humiliated? Don't make me laugh. A few months before my son died, I was killed three times; that is, I was taken out of the camp three times and brought to a gravel pit. That was my third stay in a concentration camp. Three times we were chained together, three times our eyes were blindfolded, three times the rifles were raised. I've never found out why we were allowed to live. It was a form of torture, too. The execution was supposed to take as long as possible and be repeated frequently so that we would betray the underground leadership of the camp. But the underground leadership saved us. That is why we were so hated, and hatred, Herr Blumentritt . . . Well, never mind. Between those mock executions, my teeth were smashed, my lungs crushed. I am an invalid and just about manage to do my job. But I must not let that show; the weak are pensioned off. Well, now you know everything."

I swallow several times to overcome the tightness in my throat. Too many thoughts are crowding in all at once. The force of all the horrors of existence, all the bewildering contradictions and all the monstrous acts, come down on me. I must somehow shoulder all this aside. There is a single thought that demands my full attention: How was he able to receive all my petitions without responding? I both understand and do not understand him. We are chained to each other, bitterly so; that I see. He sits down and drinks, impassively.

"Yes, but why," I say, and still find it hard to talk, "why don't you take my side, if you know all that? If it was your own son! Why this hardness, after what you have been through? Three executions, your son hanged." I know I am only stammering; I cannot reduce so many ill-assorted factors to a common denominator. We both remain silent for a while. Heiland gets up again, perches on the edge of the desk, and looks over at the piano. There, somewhere over there, he is vulnerable. Perhaps that photograph is of his son.

"We go on living as though nothing had happened," I say.

"We must not be ruled by emotional considerations," he replies.

"What kind of man have you become!"

A conversation moving along the edge of an abyss. All the same, I have enough self-control left not to speak of my interview on the upper floor of the Town Hall— that interview which hangs over everyone's head, including his.

"No emotional considerations!" Heiland reproves me, descending from the desk. "For us the main thing is— something different. Believe me, Herr Blumentritt, many things have changed. But we, we ourselves, can no longer get out of our own skins. We remain what we are. In our pockets a low membership number and in our hearts a high ideal."

I stand up. I don't want to ask him bluntly whether he is happy about all this. Besides, he would not tell me the truth. I indicate that I am about to leave. "We're always told," I say, "we must face up to reality. But, in some thoughtful moment, you might ask yourself who is to blame that reality is what it is." I pause. Then I go on with the sentence: "That those on top have tightened things to an intolerable point."

His face makes a display of indignation. I turn away, leaving him in a dead space. He wavers, he encircles me with his gestures, flashes his teeth; his breathing whistles. I feel uneasy, am gripped by fear, want to leave the house; but he still owes me an answer. Then, with lowered eyes, he gives me the answer to which there is no possible response, for it is an unforgivable confession. At the same time he risks nothing, because he no sooner says it than he pulls back. His first words are: "That is due to the man we—" But then he hastily corrects himself: "That is due to the matter we haven't discussed tonight."

Enough. I must not press him any further, must never remind him of those words. He would never admit to having made this momentary confession. But he too will never forget it. It fetters me even more tightly to him, for now he knows that I know his weak spot.

Heiland accompanies me to the door, and I can sense that he wants to say something more; his hands keep fluttering. "I'll confide something else to you," he says in the dim street light. He is pale, his eyes shifting, his voice shaking, singing like a piece of metal in flight. "I've given orders for all posters to be removed by tomorrow. They're all to be taken down—for a short time. Why don't we try to make ourselves more popular? I am going to announce a contest for the beautification of the town. That sort of thing is effective; that will win over the citizens. You'll see."

I merely nod. A year from now, everything will be as before. He only wants to prove that all benefactions come from him. But will that make him any more popular? Or will it only be a blow to those who have been deriving benefits for putting up posters? It will encourage the opposition. But I don't tell him that. I am alone in the street; the door closes behind me. I go back to the house next door. Inez has not yet returned.

Blumentritt's decision simply to leave, to go to the railroad station without another word to Inez and take the train, began to waver. He felt that events, or what lay concealed behind them, had overtaken him. He sat in Inez's living room, studied his train ticket, and tucked it back in his wallet. If he did not go at once, if he did not take that early-morning train—then he would also not reclaim his suitcase at once, would have to be careful not to compromise himself, should rather take a trip in the wrong direction for a day. Best not to exchange his ticket; he would simply let it lapse. He stood up, paced her rooms, whose furniture showed only as outlines in the dim light from the hall. He wished he could talk to himself as he sometimes did, could engage in one of his monologues, but his thoughts failed him; they would not come one by one, in order, but came in a mad rush, fell over him layer upon layer, trickled away, and vanished. So it was Heiland's son who had been hanged—was that true? Was the man whose name they don't mention to blame for everything? What had Heiland meant by that statement? How much pressure did the three mock executions exert, and the ineradicable experiences; how heavily did hatred weigh? Hadn't their talk attained a dangerous degree of candor, and what did that mean? Might it be best for him to postpone his departure? In the first place, it might be dangerous to flee so short a time after interrogation by the State Security (to say the word at last). Perhaps he was under surveillance. In the second place, wasn't Heiland, after all, one of his kind? Then again, was it right for him to skip out, leave his pupils in the lurch—what were the ethics, there? And finally, Inez —not even to see her, not a word in parting, no good-bye—and she would not be coming home tonight. In view of all this, shouldn't he postpone his departure? He needed that postponement.

He could not sit still in the chair. His body was full of pinpricks; there was a fire inside it that no one quenched, a strained feeling in his limbs. At this moment he could have let himself be bound and beaten with pleasure. He felt this pleasure between his thighs—self-punishment. He was ashamed, as always when he felt lost. Something kept him from turning on any of the lights. He rose and went for the flashlight which she always kept in the hallway wardrobe. With it, he made his way through the rooms, casting its beam on objects here and there. Inez's presence was everywhere; he could feel her spirit in the arrangement of the furniture. There was something that emanated from her and clung to an object, even one she had pushed aside at random. He pictured her turning the key of a wardrobe and opening the door, taking out a dress, closing the door again, and turning the key, which stuck halfway, the door remaining open just a crack. It was as if her hand rebounded from the door, with fingers outspread and a tendon in her wrist tensing. Her skirt swirled with the movement; she went to the chair, stooped, her hair falling forward, and with a quick, practiced motion she pulled up her other stocking—and the chair would be pushed back, moved a little too close to the curtain, so that it stood askew in the angle of the wall, and was left standing there. Blumentritt saw all that as he walked through the rooms. He pulled the chair away from the wall, went up to the mahogany wardrobe with its big doors, and was tempted to turn the key as Inez did, to imitate each of her actions. He opened the door. A few tablecloths lay on the shelves, and sheets, piled casually—two or three sheets, a girdle, that was all. He opened the second door of the wardrobe. That side, too, had almost nothing in it. Empty; the wardrobe had been cleared out. Why did she have her wardrobes empty? Carefully, he closed the doors, turned around, examined another wardrobe in the adjoining room. It generally held her dresses, but there were only two. He opened drawers, chests, cupboards—everywhere it was the same. What was the meaning of it—what had she done?

These were the signs of a permanent departure. But he could tell, from the systematic depletion of her household goods, how Inez postponed everything. This delay and postponement suited her nature. She was letting her old milieu slowly shrink away to nothing, until it would become so inadequate that she would be forced to abandon it completely. She wanted to be forced, and so she was forcing the moment to come. Because she could no longer do anything but obey. Obey whom?

He stood stunned. He felt that he had been deceived and repented having himself deceived her—almost without meaning to, for he too had been forced. Only he had thought he would find her here. So she had had the courage to spirit everything away, piecemeal. The thought became obsessive. Had she only been waiting for a sign? Was she waiting for him to give it to her?

So many lessons to be drawn from this night, so many enigmas; he had not come a step farther. What should he do? In the kitchen he found half a bottle of whisky. He took a water glass from the kitchen cupboard, filled it, and downed the whisky in rapid gulps. At first it burned his tongue, then his throat; but soon every swallow went down like oil. When the glass was empty, he poured out the rest of the bottle and took the glass into the bedroom, where he switched on the night-table lamp on the window side of the room (Inez always slept in the twin bed on the door side of the room). He lit a cigarette and brought over an ash tray. Between puffs he undressed, but remained sitting on the bed, drinking. Gradually peace descended upon him. Or, at any rate, the pinpricks subsided to a prickling sensation on his skin. He spread his legs, brought his stiff leg up on the bed, took several deep breaths. He felt warmed, but his thirst was as great as ever, even after he had finished the glass; he was only too sluggish to go to the kitchen once more for water. He threw back the silk coverlet over the featherbed and lay on his side until he had finished the cigarette. Then he put out the light. He drew the cool featherbed over him, placed his right leg at an angle, and felt a kind of leaden heat around his hips suddenly take possession of him. Then he lay quiet.

In the morning his first thought was of his suitcase at the railroad station. Then he recalled his talk with Heiland. The bed beside him was empty. He reached for the Luminal in the jacket of his suit, and looked at the clock. It was not yet seven. He got up, not waiting for the tablet to take effect.

The street was deserted. Damp morning air cooled Blumentritt's forehead. He walked along the fence, cane in hand. The briskness of the morning enabled him to pull himself together more quickly than was his wont.

Once more he passed between the twin houses that had formerly been owned by Benjamin and Paul Josua. He looked over the fence into the sparse grass, at the flower borders, at the gate between the houses. Here stood the tree that had been Benjamin's doom.

Blumentritt walked up and down, and noted with a certain satisfaction that it was too late to catch the train. Once more, as always when he failed to carry out an intention, he felt a pleasant, tugging pain in his limbs, a kind of numbness. Then he became aware that he was risking a meeting with Heiland—there was no doubt that Heiland must be an early riser. It would not do to see him again; they had parted in a state of suspended, protracted indecision, basically guarded and unrevealing, but only after minutes during which each had looked deeply, far too deeply, into the other's being. They knew too much about each other.

But he wanted to clarify things for himself, to consider what to do about the suitcase at the station, whether to call for it, and why. He had to think all that out. He walked along the side walls of the houses and then turned to the right—not toward town; he wanted to get out into the open country, where he was really alone. In any case, he did not intend to show up at school this morning.

An unpaved footpath led along a row of trees uphill toward the horizon, between tilled fields. From its highest point he had an open prospect over the valley, the town, the countryside. You could never tell by the look of a country how it was governed, whether with mildness or sternness, by group interests or by a single brain. Once more Blumentritt was struck by nature's indifference. Her serenity fascinated him.

The path led by a gravel bank. It was a cone-shaped hole scooped into the side of the hill, its opening facing the valley. He stood still, leaning on his cane, and saw himself, recognized himself down there. Limping, he approached the pit; he saw himself crossing the field, saw how his cane bored into the soft ground. He tucked the cane under his arm and tramped across the curving field, which abruptly dipped steeply to the gravel bank. Putting his cane down, he descended the lip of loose stones into the semicircle, the broad hollow which faced away from the town. An open womb, he thought. And what it must be like, he thought: to be killed here, to lay off your life in a corner and drop down upon the stones, butchered, taking over into death nothing but a command, an echo from the earth's mouth, but turned away from the town (he thought of the camp square and of the familiar corner where you laid down your life like a shirt). He saw himself standing at the pit's entrance, his back to the fields. As for the execution ground, it could only be the steep wall at the farthest corner of the pit. Any firing squad would infallibly choose that spot. Over there, then. After two steps, he stood still, hands behind his back; he was pushed forward, his gait clumsy, his left leg dragging after him. He saw footprints in the gravel, the imprint of shoes in the sand, perhaps made by workmen who had been told to leave and go home, long before the day's work usually ended. He saw them reaching home, and the children would have looked wide-eyed at their fathers, the men keeping back their anger, their wives with shopping nets in their hands. He saw the women standing patiently in line in the market, saw horse-drawn carts, clocks, the rounded form of trees, fallen leaves, worms, vermin—and far too quickly he reached the steep wall and was turned around. Beyond the mouth of the gravel bank, in which direction he was now looking, he saw the edge of a field, and the man standing there; but below the man he saw the firing squad, rifles already raised, aimed. He saw only the foreshortened barrels in perspective (aiming into a pit, into a hall). Blumentritt dropped to a kneeling position. He keeled over to one side because the stiff leg went out straight; then he caught himself with his right knee. The pebbles under his knee pressed into the skin. Hands touched his head; his eyes were darkened. The last brief respite. He thought of praying. His mouth opened. Did they shoot into the open mouth? Dim recollection of a communion: he knelt, mouth open: this is my body, this is my blood—all the bread he had eaten, all he had drunk without quenching his thirst—he remembered all that, and once again faces, arms, hands touching him. A last cry for time, time to drink, time to see, time for a last deep breath. But the respite must be over by now; the command comes, the

rifles crack. He felt, for the third time, this weakness
trickling through his body; he let himself sink back, and
already almost falling—that was it, almost falling, he
stood on the edge of the path, reeling; he stooped for his
cane, thought: Led out for execution three times. Three
times, he thought.

He limped along the path to the highest point of the
hill. He looked around. The town, he thought. The land,
the trees, the fields, flowers, leaves, animals, clouds, sun,
birds swooping to earth, tossing their chirrupings at the
clouds, faraway sounds, smoke, water, the river, a boat,
people.

His return to the apartment came as a relief to Frau
Luja, although she pretended to be greatly alarmed. "Good
Heavens!" she cried. "You look like a ghost! Has some-
thing happened?"

"No, nothing at all. I'm going to lie down. Nothing
alarming."

"Oh, it's good that you're back!" Frau Luja said, clasp-
ing her hands over her chest. "We'll put everything to
rights again—whatever is wrong, it really isn't my fault,
I know."

"The main thing is I don't want to be disturbed,"
Blumentritt replied. "I'm going to lie down now, and
will you send word, by and by, over to the school that
I'm not well."

She would, Frau Luja assured him—and how could she be blamed for not being able to? Because events hours later cut her off from the school? A good many things happened to her that morning, and she heard about still other things, and the worst of it was that she could not tell Herr Blumentritt, when he had given her such strict orders that he didn't want to be disturbed. She knew how sensitive he was about that. And so she had to keep it all to herself, and even after that woman forced her way in to see him at noon, even then Frau Luja had no opportunity to confer with her tenant. The woman virtually walked right over her like the events of the day. Frau Luja had never before seen the people of Schochern running through the town in excited bands; she would never have thought it possible for them to call out the things they did—it sounded almost like obscenities—things they ordinarily never said. Besides, even later Frau Luja could not find out exactly how everything had started. Nobody in town had any precise information. Nobody knew whether this was happening only in Schochern, or in other towns too, or possibly all through the country—this riot which had been stirred up somehow, no one could say why. There were only rumors: toward dawn someone had heard the police van. On a side street off the Fish Market someone had set a poster afire. But was that true? No, people said, and Frau Luja suddenly saw it with her own eyes: all banners and posters had suddenly vanished. But who had removed them? How could you find out anything? Frau Luja snapped up

one report that it was a concerted action by an underground ring—this was the first she had heard that any
such ring existed. Others said, and Frau Luja suddenly
recalled, that the pedestal with the poster on it had been
removed from the side street some time ago, but that on
the other hand a banner had been ripped off a public
building. But which public building? Then came more
specific news: a picture had been damaged by shots:
the portrait of a hero of railroad transportation. Supposedly this had happened behind the shooting gallery
in the Fish Market—but a few bullets from the gallery
might have hit this picture by accident, for "damaged by
shots" did not necessarily mean many shots or that anyone had aimed at it. In any case, the story could not
be checked because the portrait had vanished, and those
who talked about it asserted a moment later that it had
probably been an accident, and that the ignited poster had
probably caught fire from a carelessly tossed cigarette.
The most stubborn rumor of all was to the effect that
Heiland himself had ordered all banners and posters taken
down, overnight. But whatever was Heiland thinking of,
causing all this confusion! The ubiquitous posters had
vanished from the scene, quietly destroyed, and of course
people were taken aback. But why were they all racing
about the town? Why were they blocking off the streets,
so that Frau Luja could not even reach the bridge, much
less the school by the Fairy Fountain, where she wanted
to deliver Blumentritt's excuse? This evidently was not

the time for excuses. Frau Luja made her way back home
and took refuge in the room farthest from the square.
Let those people see what such behavior led to; even
sensible Herr Blumentritt seemed not quite in his right
mind—going on a trip in the evening and returning in
the morning without his suitcase and sending excuses
to the school! And yet he'd said he was going to a congress, or whatever it was. Frau Luja had enough of such
conundrums; she sat in her room and waited, doing nothing. Only once did she get up—that was about noon,
to answer the doorbell, and then this woman came, gave
her a hasty, shy greeting and then—the hypocrite—simply
pushed her way in, crossed the hall and opened Blumentritt's door. That was enough for one day for Frau Luja
—but she remained standing in a corner of the hall.

Blumentritt got up when he saw Inez. His complexion
had turned yellowish; it was some time before life returned to his slack features. A little uncertainly, he went
to the chair by the desk, rubbing his face. What was
the matter now, what did she want?

"I've been looking everywhere for you." That re-
proachful tone.

"Is it so urgent? You had time enough to stay out overnight."

"I took my father to an Old Age Home."

"Good Lord, how you must hate him."

"On the contrary. I didn't know how much longer I'd
be able to take care of him. Up to now I've cleaned for

(205

him and everything, but if one of these days he has only the rent from the house to live on . . ." She stood by his desk. "Don't you know what is going on in the streets? I'll bet you'd sleep through the Last Judgment."

"Nonsense," he retorted. "What could ever happen in Schochern?"

Then they both heard the noise. A strange sort of noise from the Market. They listened. Falteringly, they went to the window. They saw the people coming up through the Fish Market, a procession dissolving at the edges, seeming still uncertain of its destination. Blumentritt needed only one glance to know what was going on; he immediately began to wish those people down there would scatter. But perhaps it was too late for that. Once a core had formed, once there was a determined van, this crowd would no longer break up. Blumentritt put his hands on his cheeks. His face was quivering; he could feel it. He pressed his forehead against the windowpane. The two-tined fork of the lamp post moved into his range of vision. The crowd was surging forward toward the middle of the Fish Market. They went rather slowly; the scene looked like a march of somnambulists. And then Blumentritt recognized the person in the van: Kumtsiel.

"You stay here," Inez said. "I must go to the shop and see that they don't smash anything." She vanished almost noiselessly. A moment later Blumentritt saw her walking along the solid block of houses opposite the Town Hall.

The procession had come to a halt at the Town Hall. A

few shouts rang out from the crowd. Blumentritt thought
he could hear Heiland's name. He opened the inner pane
of the double window, then paused, stood rigid, watching
what was happening. His pulse was fluttering, he was
breathing heavily, as thought a long-lasting atmospheric
depression had suddenly lifted. A picture flew out of the
balcony window of the Town Hall. Or rather, it was not
thrown, but held out and dropped; it fell almost vertically
to the ground and only the glass broke. A girl in a blue
blouse broke out of the crowd, lifted the picture from the
ground, and pressed it to her breast; while the people
jeered and laughed, she ran off with it. From a side entrance of the Town Hall, where the traffic bureau was
located, Frau Zergaden slipped away. Two men pushed
Heiland out on the balcony. His face was flushed; he tried
to raise his arms, but the men held him fast. Then one of
the men signed to the crowd to be quiet and let the mayor
speak. Heiland evidently attempted to give one of his
usual orations: Blumentritt could recognize that by the
rise and fall of his voice. Perhaps Heiland did not fully
understand what was going on; perhaps he was unable to
grasp it; he had always wanted what was best and said
the right things, and now his slogans were swallowed up
in the reviving noise. The crowd felt that they were being
mocked. The men who had brought him out on the balcony pushed him back inside, and after a while Blumentritt saw him at the front door. The crowd greeted him
with jeers, as if everything they objected to came from

him alone. He was only a symbol for all they hated, Blumentritt realized; he too had fallen prey to the impulse of trying to find a name for the unnamable and indefinable. He too had found the name of Heiland. He had fought against him, engaged in dangerous debates with him. But now, when everyone was instinctively and pointlessly hurling his hatred against this one man—now Blumentritt felt remote, apart from and above all that. He looked down in incredulous horror and waited to see what would happen. The crowd divided and closed again around Heiland. The mayor had lost his glasses. Arms reached out, threats were hurled against him; the threats mutually supported, spurred, and exceeded one another. But with the exception of a small group, most of the people soon turned away from Heiland again—what could they do with him? The others, however, the few, were evidently determined to go to extremes. Led by Kumtsiel—where had he come from?—they dragged Heiland across the square. Part of the crowd had remained in front of the Town Hall and was demanding something—Blumentritt could not make out what they were shouting. There were no police in sight. The policemen who normally patrolled the Fish Market had presumably been recalled to their headquarters and had barricaded themselves there, or else they were awaiting orders (which would not be forthcoming) and a more favorable time to take action.

Blumentritt saw the group that had captured Heiland pushing on toward the lamp post. His numbness vanished.

Without thinking, he ran to the door, forgetting his cane. In the hall he collided with Frau Luja. She pressed her clasped hands between her heavy breasts and shook her head. He did not hear what she said; he lumbered down the steps, using the banister for support, taking two steps at a time. He hurried through the front hallway and, limping and waving his arms, crossed the street. He was not yet too late, but he saw his foreboding confirmed: Kumtsiel was holding the rope in his hand. Blumentritt forced his way into the crowd. He saw Heiland wedged among them and putting up a struggle. Blumentritt pushed closer; he must make them listen, he must wrest the rope from the men's hands before the circle in front of him closed, the circle around the lamp post, around Heiland. Vividly there came to him the image of the hanged man; it did not yet bear the features of Heiland, but of Heiland's son (if it had been his son; Blumentritt was gradually growing to doubt that, too). The group was still a few steps from the lamp post. The men were hesitating; only Kumtsiel was hurrying. This time Blumentritt was on the spot in time. But could he make them listen to reason? Would they pay attention to him? He called Kumtsiel's name, but Kumtsiel shrank away from him. Blumentritt lifted his arms and thrust people aside. He was limping worse, and he was aware of the way they looked at him, waited for him, mistrust on their faces. Who was this man? What did he want? Much too well groomed and well dressed among all these workmen's blouses and calloused hands. An official?

One of the intelligentsia? They fended him off with a mixture of skepticism and contempt. Blumentritt wished he had the gift for eloquent speaking; but he knew he had no practice in that. And so he threw himself in the men's path. "What does this fellow want!" they shouted. A few women nearby called out: "Let him speak."

"Wait!" Blumentritt cried.

"We've waited long enough—we know that song and dance."

And they turned away from him. But he did not give up. He threw himself forward, interfered—he was always interfering with something. In the press under the lamp post they could not manage to get the rope ready, could not go on with the hanging. There was a small circle of men in front of him, Heiland in their midst—his, Blumentritt's, dire adversary, whom he now wanted to save. Heiland's eyes were wide open, his head hunched between his shoulders. Blumentritt lunged toward him; their eyes met for a second. Blumentritt's cries still went unheard—or wasn't he crying out at all? Was he only imagining that he was? Was he only groaning now? His temples grew hot; colored circles spun before his eyes; but he could still see the outlines of the men, Kumtsiel with the rope, shadowy figures whom he was blocking and who did not understand what he was doing. He was not even fighting against them and for Heiland, but against the gallows. He fumbled around him, seeking support, but in the press no one noticed. He forced his way farther into the circle. And then the men decided that they'd had enough of this fellow with his mouth dripping spittle and his babblings no one could understand (the police did not understand either when, a short while later, they picked him up and carried him away). The men had enough of him, enough of Heiland, enough of all those who tried to give them orders; and since Blumentritt stumbled and fell, they walked right over him. Only for a moment he caught a glimpse among them of Heiland's face, of his eyes filled with hatred.

The shout of "Police" quickly scattered the crowd, even though it was only a small band of policemen who approached and then, seeing themselves faced by a dubious situation, quickly beat a retreat. But they arrived at the Fish Market just in time to take along what the crowd left behind: an injured man writhing on the ground. It was Blumentritt, and they were able to bring him all the way to the jail without hindrance. They caught Kumtsiel a short while afterwards.

When Blumentritt stood dazedly confronting the guard, Fenk, the man spoke to him in a highly official tone. But as he explained the formalities of registration his eyes betrayed gratification at seeing the teacher at last humbled. Fenk took the prisoner's wallet, spread out the contents on the table, examined the unused railroad ticket, turned it this way and that, brought it closer to his eyes, returned it to the wallet with the identification papers, and cleared everything from the desk.

Not until Blumentritt was led to the cell, across a damp stone floor, did he realize that his imprisonment was beginning—a state of being that refuted all his life's efforts to remain free, that reduced those efforts to minor, temporary excursions. Basically, none of it was new. A dark hallway, a whitewashed staircase, partition doors in partition walls, another dark hallway—and every step was painful. When the last door, the cell door, clanged shut behind him, not even despair stirred in him. The closing of the door was only a logical conclusion for which he had always been prepared. The moment he was surrounded by nothing but this stillness between walls, isolated by a door, by law, or rather, by an arbitrary power— the moment that was so, he thought: Now nothing more can happen to me. Or at any rate, not much more! Here he was shielded from further pursuits. All travels ended at this point. During your temporary excursions you were haunted by fear of ending here; you trembled for your security, were afraid to lose the freedom you did not possess. Now all that was over. No more fear, nothing now but the mustering and tensing of all your resistance. At last resistance had a target to aim at. If only he had his body under control.

Almost stunned by the pain which now extended from his leg throughout his body, he dropped on the cot and dozed off into a state of numbness. But without closing his eyes, without a trace of sleepiness. He stared at the ceiling, traced the marks in the plaster, let his gaze slowly travel along walls and door, and became aware that once before, an eternity ago, he had spent a night inside these walls. That was after the men in leather coats had met him in front of his parents' house. The same men, pallid, stocky. Next morning he had been transported. This time he hoped he would remain in Schochern, not be taken away. Here, he could imagine the town and what was going on in it. But enough—he tried not to go on thinking. He let his hands lie where they happened to have fallen, his left hand on his thigh, his right hand near his hip. His fingertips, gliding over the cloth of his suit, reminded him that he was still wearing his best suit, in which he had meant to leave last night. The suit must look filthy, was probably torn; but Blumentritt did not even move his head to see whether this was so. For the first time he felt with almost painful keenness the deep grooves in his face which ran from his nostrils to his mouth, pressing his cheeks close to his upper jaw. He also noticed that something was changing around him. Something was gradually altering the silence, some movement, some disturbance was floating in the air; it did not belong to the cell or the building, but came from outside. It was a noise.

The noise came from the street. The muted uneasiness of the jail, a silence filamented by vague, whispering nerve strands, was suddenly crowded out by a rising and falling noise outside the building, a tumult that penetrated through the walls and into the jailyard. Blumentritt tried to get up, and to his surprise he succeeded. He dragged himself to the wall, beneath the barred window up near the ceiling, and cupped his left hand to his ear. He could tell the direction; the noise came from somewhere to the left of the window, which must look out on the entrance to the yard. Blumentritt pushed the table over to the wall underneath the window and climbed up on it, although he knew that this was forbidden. The window was almost opaque from dirt; moreover, the angle was unfortunate, the wall too wide. He could just make out the opposite corner of the yard and a section of the prison wall. The noise came from the street, that was clear; it was increasing as more and more people assembled. He could make out individual voices, even words shouted up at the windows of the jail, directed at the prisoners. Was the jail being stormed? Why and for what purpose? Schochern's history was not exactly rich in such incidents. Blumentritt judged the assemblage outside the jail with much more calmness and composure than would have been possible had he been outside. What disappointments awaited all those people out there! What illusions of freedom of action had gripped them? Imprisonment threatened the man outside in the street, not the man already in his cell, he thought. And then: what must be the situation in Schochern? The shout of "Police" which had scattered the crowd had been Heiland's salvation. No one was strung from the lamp post—that much Blumentritt had noted before he was taken away. Heiland had been saved, but there seemed no prospect that he would return to his place in the Town Hall. His order to remove the posters meant his downfall now. Those who had rushed to execute his order would not be able to lift a finger to help him. The others, the unyielding ones—would they not have recognized his weakness?

Blumentritt pushed the table back and leaned against the wall, midway between the door and the barred window. He looked at the peephole; he knew that he was under constant observation. He imagined the eye behind the peephole, the white of the eyeball when the pupil shifted to the side, the beady eye spying on him. He wished someone would come; it was time he asked for a doctor. He must have a doctor; he could not rely on his body much longer.

The door was opened. Fenk entered. Fenk closed the door with peculiar gentleness. What did that mean? Was he entering without orders? He swung his key ring. There was no triumph in his eyes, nothing.

"I suppose you think I'm going to lace into you and play superior. Nothing of the sort." He shifted uncertainly between High German and the intonations of the local dialect. "Well, sit down. I've always treated the prisoners decent."

"Please report that I must see a doctor immediately. That's all I ask you."

"It's too bad you need a doctor now!" Fenk tinkled the key ring. The sound was painful to Blumentritt. "How can I get you a doctor? I can't, not now. Here. Cigarette."

Blumentritt automatically reached for it, and accepted the light. "I'm in pain," he said. "I fell."

"Did the police knock you down?"

"Knock me down? I fell, I said."

"If anybody hit you—listen to me now—don't say a word about it. Take my advice, it's well meant, I tell you, that's all I wanted to say. I know how it is. In court that always makes an unpleasant impression, when somebody complains about the arresting personnel—that's how it is. I can give you a few tips, if you'd like."

"I'm not asking for advice—I need a doctor, that's all."

Fenk thrust out his lower lip. "Don't you hear that racket out there in the street? There's a riot. No doctor could get through." He rattled the bunch of keys again.

"Is that all you have to tell me?"

Fenk was hurt. He displayed the sorrow of the rejected; he paced back and forth in the cell, justifying himself to an imaginary judge. "And I meant well. Says to myself: you go to him, he'll be grateful . . ."

"For what?" Blumentritt pressed his hands against his forehead. He closed his eyes.

"But no, he's still snooty. Always thought well of himself. Doesn't need any advice. But then in the end, after the last questioning, before the trial—then they all come, then they realize their situation and are grateful for every word. When I could be a lot more useful right now. Or do you think"—he turned to face Blumentritt again—"that noise outside has nothing to do with you? Maybe they want to get you out of here! But it won't be so easy—the walls are thick." Fenk was really being unusually loquacious. "Hear that again? Hear that racket out there? Listen closely! And that other noise is the prisoners beating against the doors; you wouldn't know that, you were never locked up before, would be my guess, and I bet you were making a hullabaloo with the rest today—oh well, that's none of my affair, I'm not your judge, God knows, I don't have anything to do with them that want to condemn you. Bad enough that you're locked up here just like those others who are pounding on the doors—they hit out like wild men! I've got to watch that I don't get popped on the head. I wouldn't put it past Kumtsiel—he was here before and then they let him out, but he seems to be sore at them about it. Funny, isn't it, that I first complained about you to Kumtsiel and now I'm talking about Kumtsiel to you. But who would be closer to me? You, of course. He's a pounder, I have to be just as careful about him as the others, they pound and would jump me if they had the chance. This is all I needed, just before the end."

"End?"

"Here I've been careful about everything, kept my eyes open in all directions, did my job and didn't get thrown out, treated the prisoners decent, by God, I did. Nobody can blame me for anything if things change. I always had an extra cigarette for the politicals."

"Are you scared?" Blumentritt asked curiously.

"Scared? What gives you that idea! I haven't done anything I should be sorry for. Or can't you forgive me for complaining about my son?" Fenk showed renewed grief. "If it made trouble for you—I didn't want that. And a man has to be able to forget sometimes. I want to make up for it. One hand washes the other. You're a sensible man, I think, a person can talk to you."

"What do you want of me?" Blumentritt groaned. He was at the end of his strength.

"I don't want nothing from you, not a thing. After all, you're in the soup, not me. But if you don't want my help . . ." He spread his arms wide, dropped them again; the bunch of keys floated upward with his hands and dropped again, but did not tinkle.

"Help anyone you can any way you like." Blumentritt clamped the cigarette between his fingertips and pinched it hard with his fingernails so he could smoke it to the last puff.

"Assuming you'll speak up for me some day, maybe even tomorrow." He waited for Blumentritt, the prisoner, to snap at this bait. "Tit for tat. Don't you see? That's life."

"Have you done this often?" Blumentritt asked.

"A man needs others. And if some day . . ." He waited in vain for the prisoner to manifest curiosity about what favors a guard could offer. "What's a man to do?"

"You ought to know."

"Well, then, let's suppose . . ." Fenk grew tired of wait-

ing. He looked nervously toward the door; the drumming
in the corridor had not abated. He came closer to Blumentritt, who smelled his insipid breath and the cloth of his
jacket. Stooping, Fenk whispered: "Let's suppose—now
listen closely—I take two prisoners down to the garbage
pit. One of them might be you. In today's excitement, nobody's given me any instructions about what to do and
what not to do. Everything's in a holy mess. Hear that
racket outside? Naturally I'm not going to pick any of
those hellraisers, you can see that. It's only common sense
for me to pick the harmless ones. So then if I take this
work squad down and we cross the yard . . . You understand? Not this yard—the one in back. Next to it there's
a storage area and the garages. The door to this storage
area isn't locked. We're in the back yard, see? No wall.
Then you just knock me down, jump me, and lam into
me. See? It's the chance of a lifetime for you. I won't put
up a fight, of course, and you won't hit hard, and once
you're outside the wall and in the back yard, you'll get
over the fence easy. People are already standing on the
fence—I've seen them there—don't understand why they
haven't climbed over already and come in, at least into the
back yard. They wouldn't be able to go any farther for a
while, though. There's the big gate—I'll open that for
you. Well—is that an offer?"

Blumentritt did not want to smile, nor did he have the
energy to, but something smiled inside him. As long as
Fenk with his sweetish breath was urging the crazy plan,

a foolish and short shiver of hope ran through him; it was only brief, fleeting, against his better knowledge. Even if there were the possibility of flight, it was no way out for him. It might even be a trap. Certainly there was no point in escaping—where could he hide? Did Fenk really believe that big changes were in the offing?

Blumentritt merely said: "Thanks for your proposal— but would you please try to get a doctor for me, as soon as it's possible."

He dropped down on the cot, sidewise, so that he could prop himself on his arm, and watched the guard leave the cell with tinkling keys. Between the thumb and forefinger of his left hand Blumentritt held the remnant of the cigarette, which was no longer than a fingernail. Should he throw it away or get one more puff out of the meager butt? It did not matter. Was it possible that it might again matter? For years he had not enjoyed smoking—maybe the tobacco was to blame. For enjoyment you had to be able to let yourself go. But who could do that nowadays? A dangerous luxury. Blumentritt stared at the butt in his hand. The tobacco hissed softly, the paper curled away in black flakes, a thin thread of smoke wound upward; nothing was left but the thread of smoke which showed that somewhere a tiny particle was still burning. Blumentritt threw the butt away, stamped it out. He recalled the time when a cigarette butt had meant something, ten or twelve years ago. Those were the days of home-grown tobacco and fuzzy intoxications bred from the spirit of enterprise, given fresh impetus, again and again, by hopes for better days to come—things could not possibly be worse. Everyone had memories of those years in the late forties when everyone wanted to start life anew at last. Blumentritt recalled the smoke-filled halls into which he had plunged with a desperate determination to be gay; he recalled the pleasures which he had lived through with a physical stamina now incomprehensible to him. Twice a week he had danced all night with his stiff leg. He had still felt a little alien in this town, though it was his own home town; alien in this postwar society with so many new faces and new generations—he, a man with a knowledge of horror, of which he did not speak; a man determined to go on living; a man with the odd little habits of the bachelor, a little shy, but with eyes whose dull blackness disturbed the girls.

He pushed himself up on the cot with his left hand. His arm ached; he wanted to sit. Outside in the street, nothing had changed. The crowd seemed to be surging against the gates like a bubble of air which no one was willing to prick. By the noise Blumentritt could guess that the number of people had not diminished. For the present, nothing was happening; perhaps the police were awaiting reinforcements. On the other hand, a great deal seemed to be going on inside the jail. There was a racing back and forth in the corridors, and each time Blumentritt thought the footsteps would halt in front of his cell. He became accustomed to their approaching without concerning him, and when he had ceased to expect anyone, the door opened. Fenk, in a shrunken voice, announced the entrance of the warden. A man appeared whose face reminded Blumentritt of a catfish. A few hairs sprouted on his small, gray face. Long years of officialdom had tanned his colorless skin to leather. He spoke so dryly that you felt parched. Throughout the conversation Blumentritt stared at his open mouth, as if an indigestible remnant of food were moving back and forth inside it.

"Whether that uproar outside the gate is on your account or not," the warden said, "I have reliable information that schoolboys are among the demonstrators."

Blumentritt paled. He could not understand why the warden had taken the trouble to come to a prisoner, but the man seemed to have acted on reflection rather than impulse. The thought that his pupils were involved robbed Blumentritt of much of his remaining composure. The warden observed this with patent satisfaction.

"What conclusions do you draw from that?"

"None at all," Blumentritt replied without conviction. "I have nothing to do with it. I am innocent." He felt ashamed of the naïve word.

"We'll see about that." The catfish chewed the words.

"I need a doctor."

"At the moment all the gates are shut. No one can get in

or out. The people are behaving like madmen. That can only make your situation worse, remember that. You are the prisoner; try to make up for the trouble you've caused."

Blumentritt understood. Something was to be extorted from him. He could not imagine that anything he did would make the slightest difference. Or was the warden acting on his own responsibility? "Do you have orders to tell me that?" Blumentritt asked.

"I owe you no explanations! Unfortunately I cannot do anything about disciplinary matters. At the moment we are limited in our freedom of action. Temporarily."

"Are you frightened?"

"I'll have no impudence!" the catfish retorted, but his voice scarcely sounded confident. "Normally I would not tolerate your addressing me in such a tone. But I am trying to give you a chance."

"A chance for what?"

The warden pulled the stool over for himself, but remained standing after all, looking down at Blumentritt. "I am referring to your obligation to restore peace and quiet outside the prison. Put in a word to scatter that mob. Talk to the people. We will permit that."

"I see," Blumentritt replied. He drew his stiff leg up on the cot, so that the warden would not brush against it. "Really, an unusual idea. You want the prisoners to shout three cheers for the jail and send home the people who supposedly have come to free them—or so you say; I'm not the one who says so. You're worried about your jail. You set the tune and we're supposed to sing along. Why are you worried, why should you want me to speak to the people, if you're not frightened?"

"That is . . . ! Stand up when I talk to you, prisoner!" But the warden promptly waived this order and continued: "Assuming that they would listen to you, it would eliminate needless complications. We want to prevent unnecessary damage to the buildings and the gates. Naturally we are not afraid. What gives you that idea? But you can imagine the trouble we'll have with the administration, the repairs . . ." He then recalled that this was not the proper place to speak of repairs. "All we want you to say is: Go home, there's no need of this. The courts are just; we'll serve our sentence as we deserve—something of that sort, to quiet the people, at least for the moment. By doing that, you'll deserve consideration."

"Consideration from whom? The prison authorities?"

"I see you speak the language of the enemy!" the warden exclaimed. "You could mediate. It's your last chance."

The man was afraid for his jail and possibly for himself; unlike Blumentritt, he evidently thought the building could be stormed. Only he did not want to desert to the enemy, as did Fenk; he was merely seeking some truce, would put forward a prisoner to act as the advocate of order, and hold off any action until the police came and broke up the mob. Astounding.

"You don't answer?" the catfish persisted, with a note of sadness.

"I can't do it, it's absurd," Blumentritt said. He looked away.

"To bad," the warden said. "It's a proposition that would have been to your advantage. Have Fenk call me if you change your mind."

"I won't change my mind."

"Too bad," the warden repeated. "You've turned down a good chance. Stand up from that cot immediately, or I'll have you punished."

Turned down a good chance? Blumentritt asked himself as the warden's steps faded away down the corridor. It seemed to him that these two conversations had taken place only in his feverish imagination, as though neither Fenk nor the warden had come to him and he had only talked to himself as he often did, coolly, verbosely, unreally. Now that he was alone in his cell again, between the scrawls on the walls, the eye at the door, and the noise seeping through the window, it occurred to him that only outward passivity saved you in the long run. If you moved, you were lost. Experience had proved that: he had moved once, had gone to the Town Hall, and that had been his mistake. That had been his mistake. (Or had been moved, been pushed, dropped the brick, good God, man, *wer hat dich, du schöner Wald*, moved, pushed.) Chance —no, that implied a game with stakes and winnings which you raked in or lost. But there couldn't be any question

of unused opportunities when everyone was merely following his track, just as he, Blumentritt, had been doing
until recently, following the track, just as Inez did, and
every step out of the track proved useless; neither of them
had ever strayed from that track, with one exception, with
the exception of a single journey, a journey to opportunity. . . .

On a day which ended in a shameful scene, in a cellar
hole, in a turning back. Inez had decided to go to Mainz
to visit a friend, and he had a cousin in the Eifel Mountains
west of Koblenz. Formerly Blumentritt had not understood this cousin, and perhaps he still did not understand
him; but after the war the cousin had sent food packages,
and his two children often asked after Uncle Blumentritt:
When is Uncle Blumentritt coming at last? Or so the
cousin reported, in his annual letter. And each time he
would tell his children, he wrote: Uncle will be coming
soon. Letters were exchanged; letters meant little; but perhaps it would be well if Blumentritt visited his cousin
some time. Only there were no passes across the zone
frontier, and so he and Inez chose the route across the open
country to the north of the Harz Mountains. They rode
for hours in an overcrowded local train which smelled of
fish. Not even the smoke of cigarettes displaced this smell,
and the train had gradually come to be called after its

smell: it was known in the countryside as the herring express. For there were herring across the border, and those who came back (Inez, too, meant to come back) brought herring with them.

They got out at the next to the last station. Confident in their untried luck, they joined a group of border jumpers who had taken a guide. The evening was foggy. They left the village. The guide took them to a barn and told them to wait inside while he scouted the situation. He had collected payments from everyone—and did not show up again. In his stead the border police came; probably a prearranged game, and presumably they divided the money. The group of border jumpers was taken back into the village under heavy guard, and locked in a cellar. All night Inez and Blumentritt sat among strangers whose faces they had not even clearly seen; they sat shivering on a wooden bench, pressed close together. One of the prisoners managed to escape that night. He was dressed up in an old woman's petticoats; everyone had taken him for an old woman. He asked to be taken to the latrine pit; the guard was decent enough to look the other way, and when he turned around, the prisoner had vanished. The others were held in custody until the following afternoon. Blumentritt had to carry buckets of garbage for two hours; then they were all loaded on a truck and driven to another village, where they were interrogated, fined, and released. But outside the village, on the way to the railroad station, Inez and Blumentritt decided to try it again—God knows, it wasn't easy to go to see a cousin or to get to Mainz. At twilight, this time without a guide, they set out across the meadows. They crept along, crouching behind bushes. They reached a ditch filled with water and thought it was the border. In front of them, on the horizon, seeming almost within reach, a brightly lighted express train glided off into the night at high speed. They waded through the ditch and stood, sighing with relief, feet soaking wet, in a field. Two submachine guns were pointed at them. They had to go back, cross the ditch again, with the barrels of the submachine guns prodding their backs, and so they tramped a distance, this time to another village. They spent two nights in police headquarters. But it wasn't this which so disheartened them, nor Blumentritt's fear that the attempted border crossing would be reported to Schochern. Worst of all was the way their persons were searched. He submitted with repugnance, baring his concentration-camp scars. The police made no comment. Inez never told him what it had been like for her. She did not say a word about it, only wept for an hour, quietly, without tears; but he had never seen her crying before, nor ever afterwards. She sat through the afternoon beside him on the cot in the cell, holding her legs clamped tightly together, and even three days later she would not let him touch her. Neither of them spoke of it, and when they were released after the second night in the police cellar, their thoughts turned to the ditch or the guns or to any of a number of things, but no longer to Mainz and the Eifel Mountains. They had to tramp another hour to the nearest station. Inez walked ahead, silently; once she wanted to turn off, back toward the border, and he could sense that this time she was resolved to do it once and for all, not to return. But he called her back. In the train to Schochern (it smelled of herring) they did not exchange opinions; no one on the train spoke of anything but departure and arrival times. Later, neither of them mentioned that journey. But the image of a brightly lighted express train rapidly and silently moving into an unknown land beyond the horizon remained imprinted on their retinas forever. They were back on their old track, in Schochern, in their lives; everything went as it should; they had returned and remained. There were no repercussions for him from the "attempted border crossing"; she seemed to forget the search. Neither of them was made for jumping out of line, they told themselves—without any feeling of disappointment or resignation. On the contrary, Blumentritt drew a lesson from the experience: you could not take a step off the track. It was simply out of the question; the words *chance* or *missed opportunity* did not enter into his considerations.

Were his cousin's children still asking: Why doesn't Uncle Blumentritt come? Well, he would not come. At present he was still on a tightrope over the abyss; but this time he was not in the open, hands free, balancing him-

(229

self; he was suspended in a closed gondola and everything depended on the rope's not breaking.

The noise in the street was as loud as ever. Time had
passed, but not much, when Blumentritt was led out of
the cell. The escort which accompanied him down a
number of corridors consisted of the guard Fenk, whose
face had once more relapsed into an official mask, and a
policeman. Evidently this time there would be no bids
for secret agreements. They stopped in front of Prosecutor Schunke's door. A moment later Blumentritt stood
before a prematurely aged man in his thirties with blue,
ill-shaven cheeks and a small, sharp chin. Colorless eyes
gazed at him out of a dead man's face. With a wave of
the hand which raised the padded shoulders of his gray
suit, Schunke indicated the chair in front of the desk.
A second gesture; the guard and policeman left the room.
Schunke rocked on the rear legs of his desk chair and
knocked his knee against the edge of the desk. Behind
him hung the portrait of the patron of youth, sports,
heavy industry, hiking, agriculture, and literature. On
the side wall were photographs of the Happy Future Factory, and various streamers printed with the usual slogans:
Long live the . . . and Forward to . . . and Down with
. . . In a voice that was high but toneless, so that it sounded
muted, as though it came from the air space behind the
wall, Schunke said: "Let's have the story. Let's have the
story of how you came to be arrested."

While Blumentritt talked, Schunke, still rocking his

chair, opened a box of crackers and thrust the sweet, round disks piece by piece between his jaws. His jaws ground; Blumentritt's words trickled more slowly, stopped.

"Negotiate?" the prosecutor said. "You were trying to negotiate with the rioters in the Fish Market? That in itself was a criminal act. Only I don't happen to think it's true. Besides, we have *you*; we haven't caught the others, except for Kumtsiel. He was your accomplice."

"Is this a regular and proper interrogation?" Blumentritt asked. "Why did you send for me?"

Schunke went on rocking, went on thrusting sweet crackers between his teeth. "The forms of interrogation have perhaps changed," he said. "But you betray yourself by your uneasiness; nothing is so betraying as uneasiness. You are probably thinking of the ticket that was found on you. The sentence for that alone, I would estimate, is two years."

"What does a ticket prove?" Blumentritt knew that it proved enough.

"And the baggage. The ticket and the baggage. Ticket and baggage are enough to convict. You wanted to skip out; it was all logical and well prepared. You expected the uprising. You helped instigate it. In case it failed, you were prepared—a trip across the border, baggage and all."

"It's absurd." But now, suddenly, Blumentritt felt that this affair was beginning to throw him off the rails. He was doomed; they would not credit his story.

(231

"The baggage check is stamped with the date and hour —you left your baggage last night."

Blumentritt attempted to defend himself. "I was going on a trip. And since I have a physical handicap, so that I can't carry baggage alone, I had my bag sent to the station beforehand." He thought of the books in the suitcase; he would not like to lose them.

"And what about your attempt to cross the border?"

"I don't understand."

"Have you forgotten? Ten years ago—you tried twice to cross the border illegally."

"If you know that, you also know that I did not repeat the attempt. I wanted to visit a cousin; it was during my vacation."

"This time you're not on vacation! Always assuming we were disposed to believe you, there would remain the question of permission for your trip. You should have applied for permission and you did not."

"I intended to send a message to the school. My reasons were personal. But then I changed my mind and did not leave after all."

"Did you have an idea you were being watched when you went to the station?"

"I don't think so."

"Then why did you keep looking around?"

Blumentritt drooped with weariness. "Even if I had ever intended to leave and not return, I did not have that intention today. I knew nothing about the uprising. I've told you why I rushed out of my house and was found by the lamp post. That's all I have to say."

"What about that?" Schunke asked. "Didn't you once hint that the day might come when someone would be hanged from the lamp post again?"

"I never said that!" Blumentritt knew what he meant —his talk with Heiland after the lamp post was repaired.

"But it was something of the sort, wasn't it? You spoke about—what was that phrase again?—about the law of killing. Didn't you? And yet you're trying to assert that you had nothing to do with all that's going on out there? That you rushed out into the street only because you dreaded seeing a hanged man in front of your window? Let's sum the case up once more: Your petitions to the town, with which you attempted to distract the public from more important things—pure diversionary activity, in other words. Then your criticism, your obstinacy in refusing assignments, your peculiar way of pretending to be oversensitive, which was only camouflage—of course, you were trying to camouflage your real activities. Then your prediction of an uprising, the preparations for flight, the suitcase at the railroad station, the baggage check, the ticket, your presence in the square outside the Town Hall. More than enough evidence! But all right, let's assume you still had a spark of honor in you. Let's assume you haven't been against our government." He smiled, made a pause, and pushed a document across the table. "Then sign this here. I'll give you time."

No interrogation, then, not even preliminary examination of his guilt or innocence, but instant coercion: sign something. He read the document. It was not hard to understand: a collection of clichés. He was to declare his allegiance, praise the government, its wisdom and justice, publicly take a position and call on the citizens of Schochern to follow his example, to profess allegiance, to praise, to serve.

"Why are you giving me this if you don't believe in my innocence?" Blumentritt asked.

"Your innocence? You yourself won't think much of it soon. But this is a chance for you."

"You overestimate my influence," Blumentritt said. "How much does my word count for? I don't know what you think you'll gain by this."

"You should be seriously concerned as to how to get out of your predicament," Schunke replied. "A pledge of allegiance in this situation, an open, straightforward pledge often works wonders. Or are you afraid of what people will think and say? Would you prefer to hide away? As you preferred to hide that threatening anonymous letter you received?"

"So you know about that too."

"Of course we know about it!" Schunke declared triumphantly.

"Then you have been censoring my mail."

"No, it's much easier than that. We wrote the letter ourselves. You should have turned it in, as you're supposed to do. But your honor has its limits. That's what we wanted to find out."

Schunke's jaws stopped working. He straightened up, his dead face took on some life from the effort of eloquence. "Either you sign, then, or you don't sign and thereby admit your part in the fomenting of the uprising. That's clear enough, isn't it? I'll have you taken to the infirmary. You can sign there. You have the rest of the day to make up your mind. Take a clear-cut position. It would be convenient if your statement could be published before the day was out."

Blumentritt felt that his body was more and more losing all resistance. Schunke teetered forward once more, leaning across the desk; the ruler stood upright on the top of the desk. He said: "And we will win, today! That's something you ought to know!"

He knew it. He would see Heiland on his throne again, installed and surrounded by his loyal cohorts, with the contented smile of a man who embodies more than himself, for which reason he can overlook his weaknesses. And behind the court there also stood HE who represented more than the will of an individual, HE whose portrait had served Blumentritt as a convenient symbol, as the simple denominator of what he had always been opposed to and what in the final analysis he did not comprehend. It was an impermissible simplification, he admitted, just as the struggle against the lamp post had been based on an impermissible simplification. The lamp post too would stay, and the children would go on playing underneath it, each year's batch of children anew, circling it, embracing it, hiding their eyes against the iron stem—last one home is It—and they could tap it and shout Safe, Safe! march along, take part, Red Guardman's blood is dripping, a man like an oak, Karl Liebknecht. . . .

Yes, yes, he knew, they would win, would win today, and therefore it would be profitable if he let them use him. But since Blumentritt did not think of usefulness— had refused Fenk, had refused the warden—since he did not consider what was best for him, but only the way he would be despised, and perhaps that was his last vanity, not to be despised and not to have to despise himself— therefore he could not do Schunke the favor. Blumentritt convinced himself that this was the right course (thoughts still flashed through his mind about his cousin in the Eifel Mountains, but then all this would scarcely be comprehensible to his cousin, who had only to answer his children's questions: when is Uncle Blumentritt coming?). He thought he had nothing for which to blame himself, but still his head drooped. He felt himself growing weaker. All victories were Pyrrhic victories, even those over oneself, namely those purchased by a promise of a future whose coming no one could ever be sure of (who would ever ask after Blumentritt?). He would go on living with the courage to confess to himself that everything he had done was wrong, or that he had missed something, neglected something, only he did not know what. And no one could tell him. Everyone knew the history, the connections, the symbol, in which all of them lived, but nobody knew how to interpret it. Nobody.

The prosecutor, interpreting Blumentritt's silence as refusal—and how right he was—rang for the guard. This time Fenk did not come. Perhaps they had already locked up Fenk; everything was in a state of confusion. The other prison guard and the policeman with the rapid-fire rifle slung over his shoulder led Blumentritt back to his cell. These precautions were by now altogether disproportionate to Blumentritt's ebbing strength. He barely dragged himself down the corridor. Then, at the first turn, he fell to his knee, stretching out the stiff leg, as though he could not move on without crawling on the floor and through the narrow aperture which opened wide before him. (He gave the guards more trouble than they had anticipated.) The colored circles again whirled before his eyes; he stretched out his arms and congealed to a hard, tiny point, not to be found now, lay everything aside Blumentritt drag him he won't go willingly those few steps (they had to keep a tight hold on him) and outside the chorus: choked tormented hot barking throats. He was invisible and did not feel the guard catching him and the policeman pinning his arm behind him because he thought: a trick, the dirty dog wants to escape. Spread the fingers of your clenched hands like wings, Blumentritt, damnitall (cigarettes fell from his pocket). He tried to regain control of his body; against his lips now he felt the gusts of his breathing; but his will fought against his tongue (*frommer Sagen Aufenthalt*) his will clenched again but succumbed, he struggled to pull himself up, in vain (then they dragged him halfway to his feet, to save time), and the chorus: last stanza Blumentritt you're dying but that is only the dissolution of the core to which you congealed you'll go on living you dog Blumentritt good God man—and he tumbled head first into the dark gorge.

A NOTE ON THE TYPE

❖《❖《❖《❖《❖《❖《

THE TEXT of this book was set on the Linotype in *Janson*, a recutting made direct from type cast from matrices long thought to have been made by the Dutchman Anton Janson, who was a practicing type founder in Leipzig during the years 1668–87. However, it has been conclusively demonstrated that these types are actually the work of Nicholas Kis (1650–1702), a Hungarian, who most probably learned his trade from the master Dutch type founder Dirk Voskens. The type is an excellent example of the influential and sturdy Dutch types that prevailed in England up to the time William Caslon developed his own incomparable designs from these Dutch faces.

Composed, printed, and bound by
The Haddon Craftsmen, Scranton, Pa.
Typography and binding design by
GEORGE SALTER